"Just wondering why you don't ask Kerrie to make the copies for the meeting." His words follow me. "Seems like a better use of your time, what with her being the office manager, and you needing to log last night's surveillance report."

I ignore him—and his suggestion that I'm avoiding Kerrie. I'm not.

Okay, that's a lie.

I am avoiding her, but with good reason. Because after you drink a little too much, then go down on your ex-girlfriend/co-worker/best friend's sister while hiding in a laundry room during your brother's engagement party, things tend to get a little uncomfortable. Or so I'm told.

deepest kiss

entice me

hold me

please me

indulge me

SEXY LITTLE SINNER

J. KENNER

Sexy Little Sinner Copyright © 2019 by Julie Kenner

Cover design by Michele Catalano, Catalano Creative

Cover image by Annie Ray/Passion Pages

Digital ISBN: 978-1-940673-94-3

Print ISBN: 978-1-940673-99-8

Published by Martini & Olive

v. 2019-2-4P

Sexy Little Sinner is a work of fiction. Names, places, characters and incidents are the product of the author's imagination and are fictitious. Any resemblance to actual persons, living or dead, events or establishments is solely coincidental.

CHAPTER ONE

I'M SO COMPLETELY SCREWED.

The thought rattles around in my head, and I try to shove it away. Smother it. Silence it. Because that really isn't the kind of thought a guy wants screaming at him while his tongue is in a woman's mouth. Or when her hot, little body is writhing against him. Or when his cock is harder than he thought possible and all he can think about is sliding his hands up her thighs and under her skirt, then ripping off her panties and letting her ride him until they both see stars.

But, dammit, the thought looms: *Screwed. Totally, completely, one-hundred-percent screwed.*

Because this woman is off-limits to me. Big time. No excuses. Hands-off territory.

Not that you could tell from a snapshot of the moment, because now I've got my hand on her breast, and she's arching back as I use my thumb and forefinger to tease her nipple while she bites her lower lip and makes that sexy little whimpering sound that used to drive me wild.

Apparently it still does.

Did I mention that I'm screwed?

I break the kiss, knowing we both need to take a few deep breaths, otherwise I'll end up fucking her right here against the washing machine, the smell of fabric softener mixing with the scent of sex and desire as I claim her fast and hard, just the way I want to. The way I know *she* wants me to.

"Connor, *please.*"

My name on her lips is a demand, and so help me I give in, claiming her mouth with my own. Anything to sneak in a few more moments of stolen bliss.

"Oh, hell, *yes,*" she murmurs as she tightens her fingers in my hair. Then she practically crawls up my body, releasing her grip only long enough to settle her ass on the washer lid so that she can wrap her legs around my waist.

One of my hands cups the back of her neck, but the other is on the smooth skin of her thigh, and as I briefly open my eyes, I see that her skirt has ridden up high enough to reveal a swatch of pink panties, a dark spot revealing just how wet she is.

I groan—could the woman torture me any more? —and force myself not to slide my finger up her thigh even though all I can think about is the way she'd feel naked and beneath me, her pussy hot and slick and tight as I thrust inside her.

I recall the way she bites her lower lip when she's about to come. The way her body would tighten around me, as if she could pop me like an overripe cherry.

I remember the way it feels to explode inside her, and then pull her close and breathe in the fresh, clean scent of her hair as we both drift off to sleep, her skin warm and soft against mine.

Oh, holy hell...

I'm not just screwed. I'm fucked. Completely and totally fucked.

Because this woman is my best friend's little sister.

More than that, she's the office manager of the business I own with Pierce and my brother. And won't this make for an awkward Monday morning?

But the real cherry on my screwed up sundae is that she's my ex. The woman *I* broke up with. The girl I said goodbye to for a litany of excellent reasons, not the least of which being a fourteen year age difference that couldn't be bridged simply by mind-blowing sex.

We'd admitted there was still an attraction, but we'd agreed it was over. And ever since, we've been pretty damn mature about the whole thing.

And then I'd gone and let two martinis, celebratory champagne, and a generous pour of bourbon on the rocks lead me straight into this utility room, and right into my own personal hell, all the more so because it feels so much like heaven.

I guess that's the point of forbidden fruit.

"Kerrie—" Gently, I push her away, a fresh round of desire rising when I see her kiss-swollen lips and the flush of sensual heat on her cheeks.

"Just this once," she whispers. "Then we walk away and never mention it again." She takes my hand, then slides it under her skirt until my fingertips are rubbing her pussy. "Please, Connor," she whispers. "For old time's sake? I'm so damn horny."

"We said we wouldn't—"

I don't get the rest of the thought out, because she puts her hand over mine and tugs aside her panties. So now it's just my fingers on her core, her clit swollen and sensitive beneath my finger. "Don't think about us. Just think of it as a public service. And I'm your adoring public."

"They'll know," I say, because I know damn well she'll cry out when she comes, and our friends are just one room away, gathered in the living room to celebrate my brother Cayden's engagement.

But the protest is only for show. Hell, I'm just a guy. A guy who maybe could hold his own against the flood of alcohol that has washed away my better judgment, but who is absolutely no match for this hot little spitfire of a woman. And she damn well knows it.

My thumb is already busy on her clit, and my fingers are thrusting rhythmically inside her. If she screams, she's just going to have to stifle the sound herself, because, oh, Christ, I have to taste her. Have to see if she's as sweet as I remember, though I know she will be. How could she not? After all, she's goddamned forbidden fruit, and as I start to lower myself to my knees, all I can think is how much I crave one more bite of that apple.

"We shouldn't," I whisper. One last, lonely, futile protest.

"I know." Her voice is tight. Desperate. "I know," she repeats. "We'll think of it as another ending. The final nail in the coffin. I know you said it's over, and I get that. But for right now, let's pretend it's not."

I don't know if I should embrace those words or run from them. All I know is Kerrie. All I know is this deep, violent need.

And so as my twin brother and his fiancée play host and hostess to a houseful of their closest friends, I slide my palms along Kerrie's inner thighs, then ease her legs further apart. Then, for what is absolutely, positively going to be the very last time, I bury my face between the legs of the woman who once upon a time belonged entirely to me.

CHAPTER TWO

One month later

"Leo called," my brother Cayden says, referring to an Army buddy we're hoping to entice into signing on as the newest employee at Blackwell-Lyon Security. Cayden and I are the Lyon part of the equation, and our buddy Pierce is the Blackwell part. "He's running about fifteen minutes late."

"Not a problem. I just updated the client list and the calendar. That'll give me time to run a clean set of copies before the meeting."

"Hmm," he says, as I head toward the file room where we keep the monster of a copy machine that does everything except make espresso and warm your croissant.

I pause, glancing back at my scowling brother, who looks all the more intense with his pirate-style eyepatch, a souvenir of an injury in Afghanistan. "Problem?" I ask, though I know I shouldn't. Because that one question will undoubtedly open the can of worms that I've been doing my best to avoid for the last four weeks.

"I didn't say a thing," he assures me.

"True, you didn't. But you were thinking pretty damn loud."

He lifts a shoulder in a casual shrug. "I've got a big ass brain, brother. Can I help it if my thoughts can move mountains?"

I flip him the bird, consider myself lucky for avoiding a conversation I really don't want to have, and take a step toward the file room.

"Just wondering why you don't ask Kerrie to make the copies for the meeting." His words follow me. "Seems like a better use of your time, what with her being the office manager, and you needing to log last night's surveillance report."

I ignore him—and his suggestion that I'm avoiding Kerrie. I'm not.

Okay, that's a lie.

I am avoiding her, but with good reason. Because after you drink a little too much, then go down on your ex-girlfriend/co-worker/best friend's sister while hiding in a laundry room during your brother's engagement party, things tend to get a little uncomfortable. Or so I'm told.

But this isn't about that. It's about logistics. I passed the open door to Kerrie's office not two minutes ago, and she wasn't at her desk. Which means it's just plain easier for me to run off the five copies before returning to my office to write up my reports.

I'm not avoiding shit. And despite what you might have read in *Popular Psychology*, just because he's my twin, Cayden can't actually read my mind.

All of which I tell myself as I turn the knob on the file room door, step inside, and register two salient facts. First, the room is filled with the mechanical *whirrrr* of the machine. And second, Kerrie is the one operating it.

Her back is to me, and she's leaning forward to staple some papers, which is giving me the kind of view I really don't need at the moment. Nothing X-rated. Not even NC-17. But PG is enough to get my blood pumping. The erotic silhouette of her ankles and calves, both accentuated by four-inch heels. The soft skin behind her knees—which I happen to know is one of her most erogenous zones. Her lean, strong thighs courtesy of a daily routine of yoga or biking or swimming. And, of course, the curve of that perfect, heart-shaped ass.

How many sunrises had I greeted, morning wood nestled against that perfect rear? How many times have I cupped those round cheeks on a dance floor or held on tight as she straddled my cock, riding me all the way to heaven?

Dammit.

I'm getting hard just from the memories, and since that is definitely not the direction my thoughts need to be going at the moment, I take a step backward, intending to slip out through the still-open door before she notices me.

"Connor. Oh. Hey."

Too late.

I freeze, then gesture stupidly at the copy machine. "I needed to make some copies. It can wait."

"It's okay, I'm almost—"

But I don't hear the rest of it because I've already backed out of the room. I'm five steps down the hall when I feel her hand on my back. I'm a big guy, former Special Forces, and I hit the gym every morning, run at least two miles daily, and treat myself to a forty or fifty mile bicycle ride in the Hill Country most weekends. Even so, it only takes her one hard and fast shove to land me in one of our three empty offices. She follows me inside, slams the door behind her, then stands there glowering.

"What the hell, Kerrie?"

She crosses her arms over her chest and stays silent. Kerrie is stunning—and I'm not just saying that because she used to be mine. She is a one-hundred percent looker who even went undercover for us not that long ago as a model. Now, those huge brown eyes are soaking me up, and damned if it doesn't feel like I'm melting.

I move to the desk and lean against it, not saying a word. Maybe we're having it out and maybe we're not. But I'm not going to be the one who pushes the launch button.

There's an electrical tension in the room that both disturbs and excites me. Excites, because that's the way it is between the two of us. Always has been. And that, of course, is the disturbing part. Because how the hell are we supposed to get over each other and slide back into being just friends if the air crackles every time we're in close proximity?

"I'm sorry," she finally says, which really isn't what I expected.

"Wait. What?"

"You heard me. I screwed up." She runs her fingers through her dark blond hair, the color of local honey, then simply sighs. Kerrie has a gorgeous mouth, with full, pouty lips, and I can remember only to well how delicious they taste. Right now, though, her mouth is a thin line, the corners tugging down into a frown.

I take a step toward her. I want to reach out, to touch her. But with all the electricity zinging around the room, I can't risk the explosion.

"It's okay," I assure her, wondering if she somehow gave a client wrong information or messed up one of our corporate filings. Considering she works full time, is pursuing an MBA, and barely has time to sleep, I'm amazed she doesn't drop the ball more often. "Whatever it is, we can fix it."

"Can we? Because honestly, if I'd known you'd be like this, I would have escaped through the garage that night at the party. I would never have kissed you, much less—well, you know. No matter how much I wanted it or how amazing it felt."

Everything inside me sags with her words. "Kerrie, you know we can't—"

"Dammit, I know." She moves toward me, and now we're less than an arms-length away from each other. "I know we can't be together. Believe me, Connor, you've made that more than clear. We had just shy of a year, and then we moved on. No strings, no drama. When you told me you wanted to break up, that was the deal we made, right? We swore we'd still be friends."

"That was the deal." My voice sounds tight, and I try not to anticipate where she's going with this.

"Right. That was the deal. What we both agreed to. Even though I thought you were a complete dumb ass for breaking up with me, I didn't throw a fit or whine or turn into a raging bitch, did I?"

I can't help but smile. "No, you definitely didn't."

"Our break-up was calm and rational. As neat and tidy as that kind of thing can be. And afterwards, we were still friends. Still co-workers. And everything was cool, right?"

"It was."

"Yeah," she says. "*Was.*" She surprises me with another shove to my chest. "Hello, past tense. Because now everything has changed. So why in the name of little green goblins have you been acting like a total jerk ever since Cayden and Gracie's engagement party?"

"Whoa," I said. "How exactly am I acting like a jerk?"

"You're avoiding me," she says, because Kerrie has never been one to beat around the bush. I knew she'd call me out. That, of course, only made me put more effort into avoiding her.

"Even after we ended our fling," she continues, "which was what *you* called it, not me, you never avoided me. But then we both got a little drunk and took advantage of the utility room, and suddenly—"

"You're imagining things," I tell her, because I'm a complete ass. Of course she's not imagining things.

"Don't even."

"Fine. You're not imagining things. And the answer is that I'm a jerk. Just like you said."

"No argument there. But why the sudden case of jerk-itis? More important, do you need oral antibiotics or a cream to cure what ails you?"

"Kerrie..."

"Do not *Kerrie* me. You're being an idiot. I will totally cop to having had a crush on you for years, but once we actually got together, all that changed. It wasn't just a school girl fantasy any more, and I wasn't thirteen with a crush on the soldier who came home on leave with my brother. I was twenty-three and working as a paralegal when we started going out right before my birthday, and I was twenty-four when we broke it off, remember?"

"You think I could forget?"

"Maybe. I'm twenty-five now. Or did you forget that? Because I'm all grown up. It's been over a year since you—*you*—put on the brakes. And during all that time, did I ever badger you for more? Did I whine that I wanted anything beyond what you were willing to give? Did I complain that you were a delusional loon who didn't know a good thing when it was staring him in the face?"

"No. Not until—"

"Exactly. All that time we've been friends—good friends, obviously. Friends who know each other pretty damn intimately, and that was okay. And we've been co-workers, too. And that never caused a problem until—"

"Exactly. *Until.*"

"*Until*," she says, mimicking the way I stressed the word, "we got good and friendly at the party. And after that, I told you I missed you. Missed us."

"You told me you wanted to get back together," I remind her. Which is exactly what she'd said later that night as we shared an Uber to our respective homes.

"Yeah. And I meant it. But you said no. And I

didn't press, did I? Not once, Connor. Not once, because even though I want you so bad I sometimes think it's going to drive me mad, I still value our friendship."

I want to get a word in, but honestly I don't know what to say. Besides, she's talking at the speed of light, so I'm not sure I could even manage to squeeze a syllable in, much less a coherent sentence.

"Don't you get it? If I can't have you in my bed, I still want you in my life." She blinks rapidly, and I know her well enough to know that she's fighting back tears, and my heart squeezes tight as she says, "But you're acting like one hot night in a utility room means we can't even be friends anymore."

"Maybe we can't," I say, then want to kick myself. I don't want to hurt her—that's the last thing I want—but I've been thinking about this a lot. Thinking about *her* a lot. We can't have a relationship, for all the reasons that existed when we broke up. Fourteen good, solid reasons. And then some. But after the utility room, I have my doubts about the friendship route, too. "Maybe 'just friends' won't work for us. Because we weren't *just* friends. If we'd just been friends, you wouldn't have been so quick to say you want to get back together."

"So you're saying I blew it. I opened my mouth,

told you the truth, and screwed us up forever? Well, fuck you, Connor."

I rub my temples. This is not going well. "All I'm saying is that—"

"You know what?" Her words cut me off, and I'm grateful. Because I have no clue what I intended to say. "You're right. We'll play it your way."

"My way? What do you mean we'll play it my way?" I didn't even realize I had a way.

"You say we can't be friends?" She inches forward, and I take a corresponding step back, only to find myself pressed up against the desk. "Fine. We won't be."

"What are you talking—"

I don't get the rest of the question out, because suddenly she's pressed up against me. "Forget friends. If we're going to tumble down into the land of awkward acquaintances, I want it to be because of more than fifteen minutes in a laundry room. I don't get you as a friend or a boyfriend anymore? Then I think I deserve a fuck buddy. At least then I'll feel smug and not pissed when you can't look at me in the conference room."

I know she's kidding. Kerrie is the kind who will always try to bring some levity to an awkward situation. But before I can even grin, she shocks me by sliding her hand down to cup my package.

I jump, my entire body fried from the ten thousand volts of raw electricity that shoot through me with the contact, then I push her away, thrusting my hands into the air in a gesture of self defense.

"Whoa there, woman. Let's leave some room for the Holy Spirit."

As I'd hoped, she laughs at the reference to what had been my grandmother's favorite expression when Cayden and I were growing up in East Texas. For Gran, it had been more than a trite saying; it had been the essential rule for living that we boys and all the other boys in town were expected to follow at any and all school functions. Not to mention every other moment of the day until we resigned ourselves to wedded bliss.

Naturally, every boy in the county lost his virginity well before college. With that kind of carrot dangling, we had to see what all the fuss was about.

"I'm serious," she says, and when I meet her eyes, I realize that she means it. What I'd thought was an attempt at levity was an actual, authentic proposition.

"Fuck buddies?" I can hear the disbelief in my voice. "Sweetheart, you're insane."

"No, I'm not. And don't call me that. Not unless you're agreeing, and then only in bed. You walked away. You can damn well call me Kerrie. Or Ms. Blackwell."

"In case it escaped your attention, Ms. Blackwell, the reason we broke up was that it made no sense to be together. We didn't have a future."

"Said you."

"Damn right. Somebody had to face reality. I'm fifteen years older than you. That's a decade and a half. I'll be drawing Social Security before you even subscribe to AARP."

"Since when did you start letting government pensions and magazine publications dictate your life? And it's *fourteen* years. Not fifteen."

"I'm forty. You're twenty-five. Do the math."

She rolls her eyes. We both know that for most of the year, the difference is fourteen years. But until her birthday, I win. The victory gives me little satisfaction.

"Can we not do this again?" She drags her fingers through her hair, leaving it tousled, which on Kerrie is a very good look, indeed. "I think your reasons were bullshit, but I'm not arguing them. I'm not asking to be your girlfriend. I've moved on, Connor."

Even though that was the point of our break up, I

can't deny that her words are like a spike to my heart. "I didn't realize you were seeing someone." I mentally congratulate myself on keeping my voice steady and level.

"Why would I tell you? That's not really your business anymore."

"If you're seeing someone, then why do you want us to—"

"Dammit, Connor, I'm not seeing anyone, okay? And I'm not asking you to marry me, either. I'm just saying that we had something good, then we put it away in a box and shoved it under the bed. But it didn't stay there and when we set it free at the party, we destroyed something. So let's fix it. Can't we do that? Can't we go back to the way we were, only with both of us knowing that the relationship isn't going to go anywhere? But that—for right here and right now —we're both going to enjoy this intense attraction. Because I know you feel it, too."

Every atom in my body wants to do a fist pump, shout with joy, then bend her over the desk and seal the deal with a hot, dirty, fast fuck. That, however, I can't do.

Because even though a thousand green-eyed monsters gnawed on my kidneys simply from the thought that she'd found someone else, I know that it's just jealousy, not rationality, running the show. She needs to move on. She needs someone her own age. What's between us might be fun, but it can't last. And I can't be the guy stealing her focus when she should be looking for the real thing.

She deserves more.

And I'm going to make sure she finds it, even if it kills us both.

"Connor," she presses. "You have to at least answer me."

"I want to. Christ, Kerrie, you have to know I want to."

I watch as she licks her lips, then swallows. "That means there's a *but* coming."

"But we can't."

"Yes, we can. All we have to do—"

"*No*. Dammit, Kay," I say, calling up the nickname that only I use. "Do you have any idea how hard it is to find someone in this world you connect with? Right now, you're meeting all sorts of people through work and through school. Now's your time to meet the guy you're going to end up with. And that's good, because it just gets harder as you get older. But if we're fucking like bunnies, you won't pay attention." I feel a twist in my heart, but ignore it as I press on. "You won't find that special guy if you're with me."

"Won't I?" she says, her head cocked sideways as she studies me. For so long, in fact, that I start to get antsy.

"What?" I demand, when I can't take it any longer.

"Nothing." Her smile is both resigned and melancholy as she gets up and goes to the door. "I'm just trying to figure out how a man I know to be smart as a whip can be so goddamn stupid."

And as I stand there wondering what the hell she's talking about, she tugs open the door, slips into the hallway, and pulls it firmly closed behind her.

CHAPTER THREE

MY INSTINCT IS to follow her. I want to smooth out the bumps and make everything better for her. Hell, if I'm being honest with myself—and where Kerrie is concerned I've sacrificed both of us on the altar of my honesty—I have to admit that what I really want is to hold her and soothe her.

That, however, would be highly counterproductive.

Still, I'm not going to hide from the truth. I want her. That's the thesis of my fucked up personal essay, all the more wretched since she wants me, too.

It's like we're living in our own personal O. Henry story, complete with an utterly wretched, melancholy ending. Apropos, maybe, since the famous writer—William Sydney Porter to his friends

—used to live just a few blocks away from this very office. A small house where he penned those ironic twists.

I don't know if he ever wrote a story with characters like Kerrie and me, but if he didn't, he should have. Two people, desperately attracted to each other, who can't be together. And who, if they give in to desire, will end up paying for the pleasure of the now with the inevitable, inescapable pain of the future.

That might make for a classic short story, but that's not a future I want for her. Not Kerrie.

Being with me might be fun at first, but I've known since childhood that a relationship can't survive that kind of age gap. As the years marched on, our relationship would become a prison, and I don't want to see Kerrie ending up like my grandmother, a vibrant sixty-five-year-old who lost a decade of active life to the yoke of obligation.

Growing up, my grandmother had been a force of nature in our family, taking up much of the slack after our mother left and our dad spiraled down into depression and drink. She ran our house, volunteered all over the city, and traveled the world with her friends and my grandfather.

But that came to a screeching halt when a heart

attack landed Grandpa permanently bedridden. She spent the next decade as a shadow of herself, her vibrancy erased by long hours at the side of a man she adored, but whose slow, bedridden decline stole her life.

My grandmother always told me and Cayden that it was no hardship to stay home with him, but how could she say otherwise? Once she'd made that choice, she had to make herself believe it. Hell, she had to make him believe it.

And even if that's truly how she felt, how can I move forward with Kerrie knowing that this might be her fate? I may be in stellar shape now, but combat strains a man's body, and even though I have all my limbs, I took plenty of hits, and have the scars to prove it. Maybe I'll be fine until the end of my days. But it's more likely that some injury will flare up or some unknown toxin embedded in my cells will rear its head, and I'll end up like my grandfather, trapped in a bed under a blanket of guilt because the woman I adore is there beside me, handcuffed by the obligation of a love we should have never succumbed to.

How can I risk burdening Kerrie that way?

And what if it goes the other way? Instead of being like my grandmother—trapped by the burden of love—she follows in my mother's footsteps and grows to resent the discrepancy between us. What if, craving freedom and youth, she simply walks away from the man who is almost two decades older than her, leaving me in the same way my mother left my father. A lonely, bitter man who drowned his pain in a bottle, abandoned his eight-year-old sons to their aunt and grandmother's care, and moved ghostlike through the next few years until he finally passed out after one of his benders and never woke up.

Either way, Kerrie and I are fucked.

I know it, and she won't accept it.

But I'm not giving her a choice. I love her too much to risk destroying her.

So, yeah. I'm gonna have to RSVP "no" to the fuck buddy plan. With regrets, of course.

I stifle a frustrated sigh, then push away from the desk. Leo must be here by now, which means I need to get to the meeting, sit across a conference table from Kerrie, and try to look like none of this just went down.

Should be simple enough, but I'm foiled the second I pull open the door and find my erstwhile brother leaning against the opposite wall, his head tilted, and the brow of his visible eye cocked in something that's either amusement or consternation. Possibly both.

"What the fuck?" he asks.

Apparently, it's consternation.

"Problem?" I turn right out the door and start heading toward the conference room. "Are Pierce and Leo already in there?"

"Leo just texted. He's parking. Should be up in five." His large hand—so like my own—closes over my upper arm, urging me to a stop. "Don't you think it's time to officially tell me what's going on with you and Kerrie?"

"Going on?"

He just gives me *the* look. Because he knows. Of course he knows. Not only do we have the twin thing going on, but the man works in security. He notices when people disappear. He notices when they return. And he notices the way they interact.

I, however, am not giving an inch.

Cayden clears his throat. "Let me rephrase," my brother says. "Don't you think it's time you told me what the devil went on with you and Kerrie at my engagement party? Because unless Gracie, Pierce, Jez, and I are all completely off-base, that's when you started acting like she was Kryptonite to your Superman."

"Gracie and Jez?" Gracie is Cayden's fiancée, and Jezebel is Pierce's wife. And I've been intentionally keeping so busy over the last month that I don't think I've spent more than ten minutes at any given time with either one of them.

"You can try to avoid us," he says in a demonstration of twin-related mind-reading, "but it's pretty damned obvious. For that matter, I don't even really need to know what went on at the party, because that's pretty obvious to. And can I just say that it's breaching the boundaries of etiquette to fuck on someone else's washing machine? Just pointing that out in case you missed that lesson in finishing school."

"Cute. And I didn't fuck her. Not technically," I add when he cocks his visible eyebrow. Cayden lost an eye in the Middle East, and while I've never been intimidated by my twin, even I have to admit that it makes him look like a bad ass. Honestly, it comes in handy for the job.

"Well, hell, maybe that's the problem. Maybe we need to lock you two in the penthouse at The Driskill and let you go at it like bunnies until you get it out of your system. Because honestly, Con, you can't keep avoiding her. In case you forgot, she works here, too."

"I'm not avoiding her," I lie, pointing to the office behind me. "Talking. Just now. You watched her leave."

He meets my eyes, and except for the patch it's like looking into a goddamn mirror. Only the reflection staring back at me is centered, together, and completely content for the first time in a very long time. I'm happy for him and Gracie, I truly am.

But I can't deny the green serpent of jealousy twisting in my gut.

"Work it out," he says. "And do it fast. If we want to entice Leo to join us and not the competition, we need to make sure he sees us as a razor sharp security company with a stellar reputation and an increasingly elite client base. He's not looking to sign up at Payton Place. Got it?"

I hold up my hands in surrender, and for the first time in a long time, I really do feel like the younger brother being schooled by his elder.

Even if there is only a nine minute difference between us.

CHAPTER FOUR

AS SOON AS I step inside the large conference room, I see Leonardo Vincent Palermo standing by the windows, a huge smile lighting up his face as we all greet each other with firm handshakes and slaps on the back. Leo did a tour with Pierce, and Cayden and I met him a couple of times when we were all on leave. Born of an Italian mother with a love of art, he was named after Da Vinci and Van Gogh. "But I can't paint worth a damn," he assured us. "I don't think my mother ever forgave me."

In all the time I've known him, I never thought about the way he looks. But now, as Kerrie breaks stride when she enters the room with a sheath full of copies, I take full stock of the guy. He's dark, like Cayden and me, but whereas Cayden and I look like we grew up on a ranch, Leo looks like a cross between European royalty and a classic film star.

"Leo!" I watch, not sure if I'm amused, pissed, or jealous, as Kerrie bounds across the room into Leo's outstretched arms.

Jealous.

Yeah. Definitely jealous.

What the hell, right? I might as well own it. Because at the moment, there's really no other way to describe the dark, storm-green maelstrom of emotions roiling inside me.

"It's so great to see you again," she squeals. "It's been, what? At least two years, right?" She grinning so wide she's practically giddy, and, damn me, my first instinct is to sidle up next to her, put my arm around her shoulder, and lay claim to her.

My second impulse is to punch Leo in his smug, youthful face. Because the man's more than a decade younger than Pierce, Cayden, and me. Which means he's right there in Kerrie's target range. Or, at least, in the range I defined for her.

And I'm so lost in trying not to show on my face everything that's going on in my head that I completely miss how he responds. But if his expression is any indication, he's just as happy to see her.

Fuck me.

"Don't leave us in suspense," Pierce says, as we all finally settle into our seats. "Are you accepting our offer? Or are you going to move all the way to Austin only to sign on with some lame ass competitor?"

Leo chuckles. "When you put it like that, I guess I don't have much of a choice. When can I start?"

His words raise a chorus of welcomes, from myself included. I may have felt the bite of jealousy looking at him with Kerrie, but the truth is that Leo is a stand-up guy with a good head on his shoulders. He's competent, has a solid work ethic, and he's one of the nicest guys I've ever met. He's going to make one hell of an addition to the team.

And if there is something brewing between him and Kerrie, well, at least he's the right age. And didn't I just tell Kerrie that one of the reasons we couldn't be together was because she needed to be free to go out with eligible guys? And Leo's not only eligible, but vetted by me, Cayden, and Pierce.

That's a good thing, right?

I lean back in my chair, my head telling me it's a very good thing while my heart wants to land a quick, hard punch right in Leo's gut. That, however, is an urge that will dissipate once I get my shit together and my heart and gut catch up to the truth I already know—that Kerrie will be better off in another man's arms.

I swallow a sigh. Why the hell does being reasonable and doing the right thing have to be so goddamn painful?

"—but Connor's worked with the senator quite a bit," Pierce says, and I drag my attention back to the meeting at hand, confirming which of the names on the list are clients I brought in, answering other questions Leo has related to our processes, and generally diving into the business of growing our company.

"You mentioned that you're coming to us with an active investigation?" I say, recalling the phone meeting we had last week. Leo was still debating between joining us or accepting an offer with another company in town. But either way, he intended to retain a long-term corporate client.

Leo nods. "Carrington-Kohl Energy," he says. "Brody Carrington and I have been friends since high school, and he took over as CEO after his father retired a few years ago. About four months ago, he realized that someone in the company had been stealing proprietary information and selling it. We know who was siphoning off the information," Leo continues, pulling a file folder out of his briefcase, then passing us each a copy of a thick report. "Unfortunately, he's dead."

"Foul play?" I ask.

Leo shakes his head. "Suicide. Apparently he had aggressive cancer. He knew he was dying and decided to sell corporate secrets so that his family would have some cash after he was gone. Personally, I think more traditional life insurance would have been a better option. As it is, his family's got nothing."

"So you plugged the leak," Cayden says. "But you don't know if he managed to pass the information on to the buyer. Or even who the buyer was."

"But we have a suspect," Leo tells us. "And we're pretty confident he's holding onto the information, waiting to sell it to the highest bidder." He looks at all of us in turn, his expression underscoring the import of what he's about to say. "Michael Rollins."

Pierce whistles, and Cayden mutters a mild curse.

"Rollins." I lean back in my chair. "Would be one hell of a coup to catch that man with his hands dirty." Based two hundred miles away in Dallas, Rollins is a constant fixture in the world of high finance. A man who has a reputation of having a deal with the devil since he always seems to be two steps ahead of the market. An incredible skill if it's legit. A criminal offense if he's using spies and other nefarious means to collect pertinent data on competitors and various industrial players like Carrington-Kohl.

"So far, no one has been able to nail Rollins for playing dirty, but that's partly because no one in his organization is willing to talk," Leo says. "I have some friends in the Justice Department, and they're all panting for him to make a mistake. There's no solid proof, but they're all certain that he's not only dirty, but that he's dangerous. The kind of man who kills if it suits his needs."

"Would be quite a feather in the Blackwell-Lyon cap if we can catch Rollins with his hand in the cookie jar," Cayden says.

"And not a bad launch for my career with you guys," Leo says.

Pierce chuckles. "That sounds like you have a plan."

"I do. I just need a little help." His eyes cut to Kerrie. "Of the feminine variety."

I stiffen, every protective urge in my body flaring.

"What do you mean by that?" I ask, unable to keep the possessive tinge out of my voice.

"My sister went to school with Rollins' girlfriend, Amy, who's apparently been trying to lose that particular title for over a year now, but Rollins' is a possessive, vengeful son-of-a-bitch, and the girl's scared to leave him. I won't bore you with the details, but after much back and forth, we came up with a plan. Rollins hosts a lot of house parties, and next weekend should be a doozy, since it's his yearly extravaganza. For the last month, I've been corresponding with Rollins as a high-rolling ex-Pat living in Dubai looking for a risk-free investment. He's been pitching some bullshit deal to me, and when he heard I was going to be in town with my girlfriend, he invited us to the party."

I meet Cayden's eyes and can see he's equally impressed. That's exactly the kind of resourcefulness that Blackwell-Lyon is becoming known for.

"The plan was that I'd go in with a date, and while Rollins is busy flirting with my lovely companion, Amy and I would infiltrate his system and gather enough proof to take him down. But I've hit a snag."

"What snag?" Kerrie asks.

"The woman I usually work with on this kind of

job broke her leg in a skiing accident. The job should be an easy in and out—Amy has access to Rollins' home office and I know you guys can get whatever tech we need—but I can't risk taking in a partner who's not completely mobile, just in case."

"Makes sense," Pierce says. "I'm guessing you're looking at Kerrie as an alternate?"

"Ah, yeah." His eyes dart to Kerrie. "You know the score, you're at least somewhat familiar with the tech, and you're definitely Rollins' type. You corner him for a drink, and I'm sure Amy and I will have enough time to get the data."

"I thought this guy was dangerous," I say, my chest constricting.

"Like I said, this should be an easy in and out."

"I can totally handle that," Kerrie says, shooting me a sharp glance.

I scowl, but nod. I'm not happy, but I know I won't win this one.

"Right. Good." Leo tugs at his collar, and I actually see a hint of red creep up his neck.

"What aren't you telling us?" I ask.

"Ah, right." He swallows. "The thing is, Rollins is famous for his parties. Not because they're extravagant—they are—but because they're risqué. And when I say that, I'm being polite. I won't say that we'd be walking onto the set of *Eyes Wide Shut*, but my, um, partner and I are going to have to be convincing. And play along."

His words are like a roar in my head. "Wait a second," I say, noting Cayden's amused expression as I try to process this. "You're saying that it's a sex party?"

"Yeah," Leo says, shooting an apologetic glance toward Kerrie. "That's exactly what it is."

"Hell, no," I say at the exact same time that Kerrie smiles, flips her hair, and says, "I'm in. Hell, it'll be an adventure."

CHAPTER FIVE

AN ADVENTURE.

It's been more than twenty-four hours, and Kerrie's words still ring in my head ... along with the conversation between her and Leo that followed.

"Were you serious about it being a sex party?"

"Intrigued or mortified?"

A blush rose on her cheeks and she actually giggled. "You know me. Always up for a new kind of adventure. At least we've been friends for years. That'll make it easier."

"But we have to look like more than friends." Leo's smile was warm, not leering or suggestive. Even so, I wanted to punch him in the face. *"Wanna grab dinner and a drink soon? We can share our secrets and practice looking like a couple."*

That's when she'd shot me a tight little smile. "That sounds just about perfect."

Perfect my ass.

But considering I'm the one slamming on the brakes and pushing her away, I know I can't say anything. Especially since every rational bone in my body is telling me that she and Leo really would make a solid couple.

Unfortunately, the boneless parts—like my heart and another major organ to the south—aren't feeling too rational at the moment.

That's okay. I know I'm doing the right thing. The smart thing. Staying with Kerrie might be fun for a while, but the longer we let it go on, the more she'd lose. Better to take our pain now and get on with our lives. Even if that pain, by definition, hurts like hell.

I know that. I believe it.

And yet here I am parked outside her tiny South Austin house. Why? Well, that really is the question of the hour. The real answer is that my car pretty much drove itself over here. Which means that I should put the car back in gear, pull away from the curb, head down the street, and leave her alone.

Instead, I kill the engine and get out of the car, justifying the visit by telling myself that it's my responsibility to make sure she's comfortable going undercover. One afternoon pretending to be a model around people who weren't even remotely dangerous is one thing. Attending a party hosted by Michael Rollins under false pretenses is entirely different. I want to make sure she understands the potential danger. And that she's prepared for anything that might go down.

As I head up the drive toward her front porch, my hand goes automatically into my pocket for my keys. Not because I'm in the habit of walking into Kerrie's place uninvited—that privilege evaporated long ago—but because I still half-think of this place as Cayden's house. Once a rental property, he'd lived here after his divorce and before he and Gracie got together. It's a tiny place—just one bedroom and not even five-hundred square feet—but Kerrie jumped all over it when Cayden put it on the market.

I pull my hand out of my pocket without the key and rap on the front door. *Nothing.*

I knock again.

Still nothing.

With a frown, I look back over my shoulder to the driveway. Sure enough, her car is right there. Of course, she could have walked down the block to the convenience store on Brodie Lane. Or she could have taken an Uber to go meet her girlfriends at the bars on Rainey Street. It is a Friday night, after all, and since I spent the entire workday in Waco going over the details of an upcoming protection gig with our part-time McLennan County team, I haven't seen Kerrie since yesterday. No chatter in the break room about her plans. No laughing over a stupid joke while we wait for the Keurig to brew.

No cringing as she tells me about how she and Leo are going make such a convincing couple while they're on the Dallas job next weekend.

Shit.

I really should just turn around and go home. Because Cayden is right. This woman is my Kryptonite, and under the circumstances I should stay away until I've managed to flush her from my system.

I start to turn, but the lock clicks as I do, and the door opens to reveal Kerrie with her hair piled up under a towel, her skin dewy from what I'm certain was a scalding hot shower. She's in a pair of fleece shorts that accentuate her well-toned thighs and a white tank top that clings to her breasts, the material thin enough to reveal the outline of her dark brown nipples.

My entire body clenches, and my mouth goes dry.

Yeah, I probably should have driven away. Far and fast.

And yet...

"Connor?" There's no mistaking the surprise in her voice. "I thought it was..." She trails off with a wave of her hand and ushers me inside.

"Sorry," I say. "I just got back from Waco. I had a few thoughts about next weekend for you to keep in mind while you're prepping."

She studies my face as if she's looking for signs that I'm bullshitting her. I am—well, partly—but I hide it well. After a moment, she sighs. "This really isn't a good time. Couldn't you tell me Monday at the office? Or send me an email?"

Ouch.

"I thought—"

"That you can just pop in like nothing's changed. Like we're just friends and all is hunky-dory and peachy-keen?" She glances down, frowns, then crosses her arms over her breasts. "It's not."

"I know that. But next weekend is a new situation for you."

"And I'll have Leo to help me out. He may not have been at Blackwell-Lyon, but he's been in the business for years. Or, what? Are you saying we just hired a guy who's not up to your standards?"

"Come on, Kerrie. Don't play that game. You know that's not what I'm saying."

For a moment, I think she's going to argue. Then she turns on her heel and disappears into the bedroom. A moment later she reappears, her damp hair hanging limp around her face, her body wrapped in a fluffy pink robe that's all-too-familiar to me. I rub my fingers together, the visceral memory of the soft material torturing me.

"Fine," she says. "You're right." She leans casually against the back of the couch, the robe opening to reveal the hem of the shorts and her thigh. Before, it was just skin. Granted, it was Kerrie's skin, and therefore exceptional. But now that she's taken the effort to cover it, this unintended peek seems that much more naughty, especially since I can so easily imagine what her skin feels like under my fingertips.

Probably not the reaction she'd intended...

A few more moments pass, then she pushes a lock of hair out of her eyes and sighs. "Look, I know you care about me. I know you worry about me. I know you think that breaking up was the right thing to. I get it. I do. And for a while I was handling it just fine. But things changed at the party, right? We both know that. I mean, weren't you the one who wasn't even sure we could be friends? So what are you doing here on a Friday night, Connor? Are you trying to make this harder on me?"

Her voice is tight with emotion, and for the first time in my life I'm not that chivalrous guy who always tries to do right by a woman. Dammit, my grandma taught me better. "Shit, Kerrie, you're right. I'm sorry. I swear I wasn't thinking about anything except making sure you're well-prepped."

"That's not your job. And this isn't the time."

"This is Michael Rollins we're talking about." I say the words, but I'm hating myself as I do. Because even as they're rolling out in all their efficient, reasonable, truthful-sounding glory, the man I'm really concerned about isn't the potentially dangerous scumbag of the financial world. No, I'm worrying about the hot-blooded, Italian, former Marine who's escorting my ex-girlfriend to a sex party.

When you put it that way...

"You need to be careful." My words are stern.

She cocks her head, her mouth curving into a knowing grin as she asks, "Are we talking Rollins, the situation, or Leo?"

I want to retort, but considering she's nailed me, there's not much to say.

Kerrie, however, is not similarly stymied. "I never wanted to break up with you. But now you're making me think that maybe your lame ass decision was the right one. I mean, you must be too old for me, right? Because I swear, you're acting more like my father than a boyfriend."

"I'm not your boyfriend."

A muscle in her cheek twitches. "No, you've made that clear. You're not acting like a co-worker, either. A co-worker would call or email or wait until Monday."

"Is it a crime for me to still care?"

"*Yes.* No. Hell, I don't know." She meets my eyes, and I see something that might be sympathy reflected back at me. "Listen, Connor, I know you're worried, but I'm going to be fine. I'm just a prop, just the girl Leo needs on his arm. You know that as well as I do. Leo's the one who'll be doing the heavy lifting, and we both know he's well-trained. Really," she adds gently, "I'll be fine."

My heart twists from nothing more than the tone of her voice, and I feel like a heel again. I didn't come here to remind her that she cares for me or to make it harder on her.

Which begs the question of why I came at all. Because she's right. Everything I came to say could easily wait until Monday.

I'm trying to decide if I should own up and tell her that I was wrong. That we *can* be friends. More, I want to. Yesterday in the office was a stumbling block, but despite what I said, even though I've pushed her out of my bed, I don't want to push her out of my life.

That's what I *want* to say. But I don't get the words out because as I'm still playing the tune in my head, she clears her throat, then nudges me with her voice. "Um, listen, can we talk on Monday? Or later this weekend if you think we need to. It's just that I need to go get ready, so..."

She trails off with a slight nod toward the door.

I glance at my watch—almost seven. Kerrie habitually spends her nights at home in PJs and a robe. "You're going out?"

"Well, um, yes. *Yes.* I am. It's Friday, and I have a date." She licks her lips. "So if you could go, that would be great. It would be kind of awkward for the two of you to bump into each other, don't you think?"

"Who is he?" I tell myself I'm happy she's dating again. I force myself to believe that the only reason I'm asking the little prick's identity is so that I can run a quick check on lover boy. For Kerrie's safety, of course.

I can tell from the look on her face that she knows exactly what I'm planning.

"We're not playing this game." Her voice broaches no argument.

"Right. I know. I'm sorry." I move to her front door and rest my hand on the knob. "I'll get out of your hair." I want to tell her she looks great, but considering where this relationship needs to go—specifically, nowhere—I keep my mouth shut and tug open the door.

And standing right there, his hand raised to knock, is Leo.

CHAPTER SIX

"CONNOR! Hey, buddy, good to see you."

Leo gives my shoulder a friendly pat as he steps past me to enter the house, either not caring or not knowing that his date's ex-boyfriend is standing right in front of him.

Is this a date-date, I wonder. Or are they just doing what they'd talked about and getting comfortable with each other so that they can pass themselves off as intimate.

I glance over in time to see Leo brush a kiss over her lips without appearing the slightest bit self-conscious.

That, I think, *is clue number one.*

"Sorry I'm not ready," Kerrie says. "Connor and I got to talking."

"No worries. We have time before the reservation."

Reservation. That sounds like more than a rehearsal to me. Let's call that *clue number two.*

Fucking, Lame-ass Clue Number Two.

I shake my head like a dog, warding off these damnable thoughts.

"You okay?" Leo's squinting at me.

"Fine. Just a lot of stuff on my plate." I toss my thumb over my shoulder to indicate the door. "I should head out. And I know you two need time to, ah, rehearse."

"Oh," Leo says. He looks up at Kerrie's beaming face, then murmurs. "Rehearse. Yeah." He takes her hand. "That's a good word for it."

My stomach twists, but I remind myself that this is good. Leo's a stand-up guy. This is what I want.

My brain knows that. The rest of me just hasn't caught up with reality.

Which is why I need to leave before I kill the son-of-a-bitch. "Right," I say, my voice brisk and cheerful. "I'm out of here."

I'm at the door when he calls out, "Actually, can you stay a bit longer? There's something we need to discuss. About the Rollins case, I mean."

My brow furrows as I look to Kerrie, who shrugs.

Obviously she doesn't know what's going on any more than I do.

I follow both of them to the living area, which isn't a long trek in the tiny house. As Kerrie settles onto the floor, her back against the sofa, I cop an armrest. Leo stands in front of us, his hands shoved deep into his pockets, his expression unreadable.

"Just spit it out," I say, curious now.

He draws in a breath, and I see a flicker of consternation cross his face. "As much as I'd enjoy this assignment, there's been a change in plans."

I turn to Kerrie, only to find her looking back at me, clearly just as confused.

"What are you talking about?" I ask.

"Remember how I told you that my sister went to school with Rollins girlfriend, Amy? The one who's been helping us? Well, turns out there's a picture of me in Rollins' office."

"How?" I ask. "According to the briefing notes, Amy and Rollins weren't together until well after she graduated."

"True," Leo says. "And that's part of why it never occurred to me that this might be a problem. But apparently Amy had a photo collage of her made for Rollins about seven months ago. To celebrate the anniversary of their first date. Back when she didn't realize that Rollins was the spawn of Satan."

"I still don't understand what the problem is," Kerrie says.

"The problem is that Leo's picture is part of that collage." I meet his eyes. "Isn't it?"

"Afraid so." His hands are still in his pockets, but now his shoulders rise and fall in an expression of frustration. "Mae and I went with Amy to a concert in Zilker Park. We were all screwing around, and someone took a picture of the three of us. I'm right in the middle, larger than life, an arm around both girls' shoulders."

"Which means that Rollins might recognize you," Kerrie says.

"He probably won't, but we can't take the risk. If we'd known, I could have shifted my cover story. Worked Amy in as an old friend. But changing it up now is too risky."

Kerrie's brow furrows. "So what do we do?"

"Same plan, different players," Leo says. "I just got off the phone with Cayden and Pierce. Called you," he adds, looking at me, "but it rolled to voicemail."

I pull out my phone. Sure enough, there's a missed call.

"Consensus was, as the only single guy in the company not on Rollins' radar, you're our man. And Kerrie, of course, is still the girl. And you two have been friends forever, right? So the fake relationship thing won't be a problem."

"No," I say, my chest suddenly tight, but whether with dread or anticipation, I really don't know. "That won't be a problem at all."

"Wait, wait," Kerrie says. "Won't Rollins realize that Connor's voice is different?"

Leo shakes his head. "I doubt it. Our voices are pretty close in timbre. And most of the time, Rollins and I communicated by email. Made it easier, what with the time difference. The one time we did talk, it was on speaker and I turned on a static generator. We could barely hear each other." He grins, looking pleased with himself. "I like to plan for all contingencies. Guess this time that practice came in handy."

"No kidding," I say.

"So that's the plan," Leo says, looking between Kerrie and me. "All good?"

I know that I should object. Right now really isn't the best time for Kerrie and me to be undercover at a sex party. But all I say is, "Yeah. Sure."

I am, after all, a professional.

Besides, this might turn dangerous. And in that case, I'm the only one I truly trust to keep Kerrie safe.

"Excellent," Leo says. "So we've got about a week before the party. We can start briefing tomorrow, and I'll get you access to my fake Dubai email account, all our correspondence, and the rest of it."

I nod, not worried about getting up to speed. I've taken on more complicated personas for undercover work. No, my only concern is sitting right next to me. But—again—*professional*.

And that, of course, is going to be my buzzword for the entire operation.

Leo reaches down and offers Kerrie his hand, helping her up. "Rain check okay?" He's still holding her hand. "I want to make sure everything in my head is in a brief for Connor."

"Of course. We can do dinner some other time."

"And you two should probably go out," he adds, nodding at me. "Play the boyfriend/girlfriend game. You want it to look convincing."

"Yeah," I say, acknowledging that despite my best efforts to stay away from this woman and give her the space to move on, Leo Palermo has just shoved both of us into the rabbit hole.

CHAPTER SEVEN

ALTHOUGH THE IMAGE of Kerrie's hand intertwined with Leo's stays in my head for the next few days, I get no further clues as to whether or not there's anything brewing between the two of them. Maybe it was just a friendly, casual gesture. Or maybe they're both damn fine actors in the office who fuck like bunnies once the workday is over.

I tell myself that would be just fine. Great in fact. They'd make a cute couple.

I am, of course, a lying son-of-a-bitch.

Fortunately, I don't have much time to ponder. Instead, I'm focusing on the role I'll be playing. John London. An ex-Pat high roller looking to pad his pocketbook even more. Back in the states for a whirlwind trip to see friends and business advisors, his young and pretty trophy girlfriend—Lydia—at his side.

And no, I'm not blind to the irony. For this particular assignment, the fifteen years between us works to our advantage.

One week is pretty tight prep time for a Thursday-to-Sunday, no-respite undercover assignment. But Leo's a consummate professional, and he's been working closely with both me and Kerrie, drilling us over and over again on our cover stories, the details of how I made my fortune, a description of my office in Dubai, the backstory of how I ended up living and working in that part of the world, how I met Kerrie—sorry, *Lydia*—and on and on and on.

The three of us have been more or less attached at the hip for days. Certainly, we've been locked in close quarters, having commandeered the bigger of the office's two conference rooms as our own. The downside is that I never have a moment to myself as we cram, study, and stay in character. The upside is that we've thoroughly trounced whatever insecure demon had me avoiding Kerrie.

"I guess my evil plan worked," she says as we're taking a break to wolf down a quick lunch, and Leo had stepped out to take a phone call.

I grin. "I always knew there was a touch of evil inside you. Those wicked, wicked ways of yours."

"Not wicked," she retorts in that silky tone I know so well. "Naughty." For a moment, I'm caught in her sultry gaze. Then she grins broadly, laughs, and says, "Isn't this so much better?"

It takes me a moment to mentally switch gears, and longer for my body to drop back to a normal temperature. I, however, reveal none of that as I say, "Better?"

"Than you avoiding me. It's been nice working side-by-side with you again. I've missed you."

My gut twists. "Kerrie..."

"No, no. It's okay." She lays her hand on mine. "This is what I meant. My evil plan. I mean, I didn't really have a plan, of course. But I think this job will be good for us. I feel like it's already repairing our friendship. Don't you?"

I glance at where her hand rests on mine. She's right, of course. We'd been friends for years before we were lovers, and I've always respected the hell out of her. She's smart and loyal and sweet and funny. She's never met a stranger, and she goes after what she wants. I should know—she went after me, didn't she?

Not that I put up much of a fight. Hell, once I

saw her as a woman and not the thirteen-year-old girl she'd been when we met years before, I wanted her, too. For that matter, I still do. Only now I'm exercising the self-control that I didn't have back then.

And, yes, I regret the month I spent avoiding her. I blame it on Adult Onset Adolescence caused by an unexpected make-out session. Which is to say that I got lucky in the utility room, and like a thirteen year old boy who doesn't have a clue how to deal, I basically hid under the metaphorical covers and tried to pretend the world—or at least the girl—away.

Which is especially ironic considering that we broke up because I'm so much older. Apparently *older* doesn't always translate to maturity. Who knew?

"Connor?"

I hear the worry in her voice and look up, realizing I'm still staring at our hands.

"You do agree, right? That this has been good for us."

"Yes. Yes, sorry. My mind is all over the place, but I do. I absolutely do."

"Good." She gives my hand a quick squeeze, and I wish that I didn't feel the contact so deeply. But I do, and I hate myself for the fantasies that whip through my head, each and every one flying by on guilt-ridden wings. Because what right do I have to fantasize? I'm the one who called it quits, after all.

Kerrie, however doesn't seem to notice my mood shift. And when Leo returns she snatches her hand off mine, flashes him a wide smile, and offers him her bag of potato chips.

Jealousy, thy name is Connor.

I force the green monster back into his pen and knuckle down, trying to ignore my growing suspicion. And as more hours turn into more days, it becomes easier. Because Leo is a relentless taskmaster, and there's no room to think about anything other than the operation.

Hopefully all our intensive prep is overkill, but the alcohol will surely be flowing at the party, which means that tongues will be loose. And while we can try to limit how much we drink, we can't refuse to imbibe without causing suspicion.

Considering the nature of the party, there are other things we can't avoid doing without causing suspicion. And, damn me, I can't deny the unwelcome anticipation growing inside me.

I shouldn't want it. I should tell Kerrie that no matter what, we're going to fake it.

But faking it could put us both in danger. And—

hell, I have to at least admit it to myself, right?—I do want it. I want *her*. Despite everything I know is right and every solid reason I have for not ever touching her again, this job feels like a gift. A strings-free way to have Kerrie beside me—*with* me—one last time

And that, of course, is what makes this mission truly dangerous.

For days, I've been expecting Kerrie to make some comment—a tease about how we're fated and there's no way I can truly walk away from her because the universe will just draw us back together. But that comment doesn't come.

I tell myself that's good. That she's healing. That I want her to move on.

Sure, there's still a dull ache that surrounds my heart, like the phantom pain of an amputated limb. But that's okay. I survived multiple tours in the Middle East. I can survive heartache.

Hell, yeah, I can.

The party is Friday to Sunday, and I work late Thursday to clear my plate of all my other work. We're both taking burner phones—Pierce, Cayden, and Leo have the contact info — but nothing that gives away our true identities. We don't want any identifying information on us if we're caught red-handed, but I wouldn't put it past a man like Rollins to ransack his guests' belongings looking for ammo to fuel a blackmail scheme.

It's almost seven by the time I finish. Leo left just after noon for a lunch meeting with a client who's in town on other business. Before that, we went over the tech one last time—we got some seriously cool new gadgets for this job from our most innovative supplier, Noah Carter over at the Austin Division of Stark Applied Technology—then Leo wished me luck and told me to watch out for Kerrie. And to nail Rollins.

I assured him that was my plan.

Cayden and Pierce left later after another quick debrief. They're both serving as backup, but they're as up to speed on the job as Kerrie and I are.

Now, I'm heading home for a quick workout and a full night's sleep. Considering the reputation of Rollins' parties, I'm not sure I'll be getting much shut-eye until Sunday night.

Although she's our office manager, lately, Kerrie's been working more from the reception desk in our small lobby than from her office. We've had four receptionists over the last six months and at this point, we're all pretty convinced that the post is cursed.

I expect to see her there, buried in either briefs for the operation or spreadsheets for the business. But the computer is shut down and the desk is locked tight.

Which means that Kerrie left for the night without even a goodbye.

I tell myself she probably didn't want to disturb me, but the truth is that her silent departure bothers me more than any interruption would. It's just not like her.

Still, I don't want to read too much into it. She undoubtedly still needs to pack. And I'm sure she wants to get a full night's sleep, too.

I lock the office, then take the elevator to the lobby, feeling a little bit hollow and oddly alone.

The plan is for me to pick up Kerrie at ten tomorrow morning. It's about a three-hour drive to Rollins' ranch in North Dallas, and if we stop for lunch along the way, we should get there right at the appointed hour of two. That gives us time to get settled in our room, possibly meet up with Amy, and become familiarized with the layout of the place before the welcome cocktails at five.

We have the blueprints and Amy's description, of course. But I'm not willing to take anything for granted. Especially since Kerrie is with me, and no matter how much of an in-and-out job this is supposed to be, her presence on an operation means that her safety is on the line. And that's not something I'll ever take lightly.

I cross the lobby, then step out onto the sidewalk that runs in front of our building at Sixth and Congress. The street is bustling, and I join the fray, eager to get home.

Like Kerrie, I moved not too long ago. When I first came to Austin, I lived in a small house in Central Austin, but used some of my trust fund to buy one of Austin's early downtown condos as a rental property. An investment banker, our dad might have spiraled down after our mom left, but he was always careful with his money, and after his death, our grandmother managed the trusts until Cayden and I were old enough. Not a huge sum, but enough for a nice down payment on the condo, which I turned into a shiny profit a few months ago when I sold it, then upsized to a bigger condo in a nicer building.

Now I'm living the downtown urban lifestyle in a fabulous two story corner condo with a view of the river. And my original Crestview bungalow has been converted from my primary address to a rental that brings in a tidy monthly income.

Dad may not have had the wherewithal to survive heartache, but he left his sons a nice legacy. His grandkids, too, since I'm one-hundred-percent certain that Cayden is waiting for kids before spending a penny of his still-untouched trust.

Unlike my brother who prefers a sprawling house with a yard that requires constant upkeep, I love my condo and its location. My view is exceptional and requires no effort from me. The lobby is always tidy, and if there's no food in the refrigerator, all I have to do is go out through the lobby door, turn left, and I can grab some supplies at the nearby Royal Blue Grocery. Turn right, and I can eschew cooking all together and grab a sandwich at my favorite deli. Not to mention all the options open to me if I walk even a few blocks.

My usual after-work routine is to head south down Congress Avenue, popping into Brew for coffee before I head home. They know me there, and I kick back, log onto my favorite news app, and spend half an hour catching up on the world outside my little circle.

Then I head home, change into shorts, and go for a quick run around the river. After that, my routine gets fuzzy. Before, I tended to stay in with Kerrie. We'd cook, maybe watch a movie, maybe read. Often we'd take nighttime strolls along the river. And we always ended up in bed. Sometimes wild and desperate. Others times, slow and easy. Hell, sometimes we just held hands and talked.

Now, I tend to watch a lot of reality TV. What can I say? I sacrificed the bliss of those nights for the promise of her future. I don't regret it. But if I'm being honest, I have to admit that I don't like it.

Scowling, I cross the street and head toward Brew. Really not the kind of thoughts I want in my head while I'm trying to make a clean break. Especially since that break just got messier. Because even if we can fake what happens behind closed doors, we can't pull off even pretend intimacy without physical contact.

Damn Leo and his sister and Amy.

But at the same time, I'm glad it's me and Kerrie going, and not her and Leo. I'd be a jealous fool waiting behind in Austin for them to complete this operation. This way, at least, I have a few more moments with her. A few more touches and kisses. A few more memories.

Just a little bit more to hold onto after we get back and finally, truly, cut the lingering ties between us.

I've hit Brew at just the wrong time, and the line

for coffee is out the door. I wait, using the time to scroll through messages on my phone. Once the line moves enough for me to enter, I glance automatically around the room. Occupational hazard—I'm always assessing my surroundings.

Right now, my assessment reveals Kerrie. And, fuck me, she's sitting at a table with Leo, deep in conversation.

Obviously, they're doing prep work, and the green demon in my gut needs to chill. I'm trying to tame the jealous beast, when Kerrie pushes a strand of hair out of her eyes, and in the process turns in my direction. She's looking right at me, but her eyes are unfocused, and though I lift a hand in greeting, she turns away as if I'm nothing more than a shimmer in the air, then takes Leo's hand as she laughs at something he's said.

My gut tightens, and in that brief moment, I have a sense of what it will really feel like when there's a new man in her life. I don't like it, but I can't change it.

Because I know that my decision is the right one.

I just never expected that doing the right thing was going to hurt like hell.

CHAPTER EIGHT

"WE'LL STOP at George's for lunch, right?" Kerrie asks as the soundtrack to *Wicked* blares from the Mercedes S-Class sedan I rented for the trip.

Correction: The Mercedes that John London rented upon his arrival in Austin last night.

I reach over and turn down the volume. Kerrie's musical taste runs to Broadway musicals, classic country, and hip-hop. My girl is nothing if not eclectic.

We've been driving north on Interstate 35 for the last forty-five minutes and we're about halfway to Waco. We've already run through *Into the Woods*, and Kerrie's already downed half a bag of jelly beans.

As I glance over at the bag in her lap, she flashes

a grin, then grabs a handful of the candy and holds it out to me. "Share?"

"Keep eating those and you won't want George's." The long-established Waco dive is famous for its burgers and beer. And for good reason.

"It's not the burger I want," she says, adding a sultry lilt to her voice. "It's the Big O."

"Kerrie..."

She laughs. "That's Lydia to you, bud. And I think that under the circumstances I'm entitled to a little naughty talk. Gotta stay in character, right? Besides, all I want is a beer."

"Uh-huh." The Big O at George's is a glass of beer. A very big glass of beer that has sustained many Baylor University students over the years.

She rolls her eyes. "Your mind is *so* in the gutter."

"Fine. Lunch it is. And you can have all the Big Os you want."

She reaches over and gently presses her palm on my thigh. "Now you're talking."

"Kerrie..."

"I'm just teasing," she says, but she pulls her hand back. "I mean, we are still friends, right?"

"Of course we are." As hard as it is, I can't imagine not being her friend, no matter what I might have said in desperation a few days ago.

"Well, I'm Cayden's friend, too, and we flirt."

"Yeah, but you never slept with Cayden. Did you?"

I get her eye roll in response. "All I'm saying is that I don't want to lose your friendship. Am I attracted to you? Of course. Would I jump all over you and dive head first into my fuck buddy plan if you said go? Absolutely. Am I going to push you on it? No."

She shifts in her seat so that she's facing me more directly. "I'm all grown up, Con, and I'm moving on. And I'm mature enough to talk about this reasonably."

She's still talking, but my mind stopped processing after *moving on.* Is she?

I can't help but think of Leo and the image of the two of them laughing and talking in the coffee shop. And me, right there, but completely apart.

I don't like it. But what the hell am I supposed to do about it? Especially considering I'm the one who told her to move on in the first place.

When I tune back in, I realize I've lost the thread of the conversation. "Sorry. What?"

"I said that I don't want to lose having you in my life. You weren't just my boyfriend, you were my friend. Probably my best friend. We're not going to toss that all away just because we're going through an awkward period, are we? We can get past this. And in a few years when I have kids, I want them to adore their uncle Connor as much as I do."

Mentally, I cringe. And despite the fact that her last bit really twisted the knife, I can't deny that her speech makes sense, and I tell her so.

What I don't tell her is that her words only emphasize all the reasons I love her. Kerrie is one of those people who sees the world with crystal clarity. And for a man who works in a world where people usually aren't who they seem, that's a pretty damn refreshing trait.

"I'm sorry," I say as we speed north on the highway, leaving Belton and Temple in our wake.

"For what?"

"For knowing that what you just said is true. For believing it since the first moment I walked away. And for still acting like an asshole and avoiding you."

"Oh." She breaks into a wide smile, looking happier than I've seen her in days. "You're forgiven," she says. "On one condition."

"Buy you a beer?"

"Buy me two."

————

I don't know about Kerrie, but I'm still stuffed when
we reach the turn off to Michael Rollin's North
Dallas ranch, over a hundred miles from where we
grabbed lunch.

Kerrie's been dozing—she's a lightweight with
alcohol anyway, and two beers did her in—and I've
been cruising along dead cold sober with only my
racing thoughts to occupy me. Everything from
memories to past drives with Kerrie to worries about
how the hell we're going to share a room without her
ending up naked and hot beneath me.

Be strong, Connor.

That's all well and good. But tonight, I'm John.
And God only knows how much willpower *that*
man has.

I turn off the asphalt and onto the crushed stone
drive leading up to the huge mansion that sits on
what I'm guessing is a four-hundred-acre ranch. The
land is flat and raw and beautiful, green from the
frequent summer thunderstorms, and dotted with
color from wild flowers. I see horses and cattle and
goats and a few critters I can't identify from this
distance.

I drive slowly, taking it all in and giving Kerrie a
chance to wake up beside me.

"It's pretty," she says. "And that house..."

"I'm not sure that's a house. I'm thinking it's an embassy."

She laughs, but it's true. The red brick and white-column two-story ranch house is huge and stately and looks like it could house the key players of a small country. Michael Rollins clearly has the kind of money that normal peons like me can't even wrap their heads around. John London, however ... well, to him this is old hat.

I force my face into a bland expression as I glide the Mercedes to a stop in front of the door. A young valet in jeans, cowboy boots, and a starched white button down hurries to my door as another opens the door for Kerrie. Or, rather, for Lydia.

"Ready, Lydia?"

"Ready, John."

I give the keys to the valet and pop the trunk. Our bags are whisked efficiently away, presumably to be searched before they arrive in our room. Ditto the car. I'm not worried. We packed and traveled in character.

I doubt they'll run prints since the car is so obviously a rental and must have quite a variety of prints on the interior, but if they do, they'll come up empty. Prior to setting out, we wiped down our luggage and then both used liquid latex and a thin layer of powder on our fingertips to conceal our prints during the drive.

I take Kerrie's hand as we walk together toward the door. Both because I imagine she wants the support, but also because I want to confirm that she remembered to rub off the telltale latex. She has, and I presume the remnants are now unrecognizable in her purse or pockets.

Probably overkill, but I'd rather overdo caution than find myself screwed.

The front door opens as we're walking up the steps, and Michael Rollins steps out, tall and commanding, with blonde hair, piercing blue eyes, and a wide mouth. He stands with his feet just slightly apart, and one hand behind his back. He looks like a king about to give a speech, and I have a feeling that's the way he thinks of himself. He's the man in charge, and the rest of us need to just fall in line.

This weekend, that's the plan. Get in, make nice, and draw absolutely no suspicion.

"John London," he says, extending his hand to shake. "I would recognize you anywhere."

I make it a point not to react. Leo had already papered the John London persona for anyone who might be searching the internet. But he'd included no pictures. Last weekend, we had our media-tech consultants upload some fake files and images for Rollins to find on the chance he was looking. Apparently he was.

"And you must be Lydia," he adds, his voice full of charm and charisma.

"I sure am," Kerrie says, letting her natural Texas twang shine through. "I just love your place. I've been to Dallas many times, but I never even knew there was so much ranch land this close to the city."

"Most of it's been developed. I'm holding out," Rollins says, still clutching Kerrie's hand as he looks into her eyes. "I like my privacy."

She giggles, and I want to punch him. A reaction that doesn't really bother me. I do my best work when I think the mark is an asshole. Clearly, I'm going to excel at this job.

Rollins leads us over the threshold and into an elegant foyer. It pushes toward garish—hell, it crosses the line—as does what little of the rest of the house I can see through the archways leading to the adjoining rooms. But none of it seems erotic or decadent or remotely like what I imagined the forum for a sex party would look like.

Apparently Kerrie is thinking the same thing,

because she smiles, revealing a dimple, and says, "It's a lovely home, but not what I was expecting."

"No?"

She lifts a shoulder. "I guess I was picturing it with ropes and chains. Or at least red satin sashes. I've never been to this kind of party before."

She's flirting with him—which is what she's supposed to do. The plan is for her to distract Rollins to give Amy and me time at his computer. But even so, that flirtatious lilt aimed in his direction acts on me like fingernails scraping a chalkboard.

He hooks his arm through hers and leads us into a living area. "I'm honored to be the one popping your party cherry," he says, making me roll my eyes and Kerrie titter. "But I assure you that by this evening the house will have a much more sensual allure."

"I can't wait."

He starts to put his arm over her shoulder, but Kerrie gently breaks away and returns to my side. I slide my arm around her waist and pull her close, feeling ridiculously smug.

"What's the dress code tonight?" Kerrie asks. She's already chastised me for not thinking to find out from Amy, forcing her to pack for contingencies ranging from slutty to sensually formal.

"Elegant," Rollins says, going to a wet bar and offering us each a drink. We both take a bourbon, and when he puts Kerrie's in her hand, Rollins adds, "Of course, we will undoubtedly loosen up later in the evening. If formal wear seems too restricting."

"Right." Kerrie smiles, her cheeks going red.

"My Lydia is an innocent," I say, brushing the pad of my thumb over her lips.

"That's deliciously sweet." He runs his gaze possessively over her, and though she smiles, I see the fire in her eyes. Under other circumstances, she'd slap his face.

"So, do we have to wear masks?" she asks.

"Not at all, though you certainly can if you want to. Just think of it as a cocktail party where everyone skips the social niceties and goes straight to getting to know one another. Intimately. The idea is to be comfortable. Play. Explore. Or just watch, if that's your particular predilection." He steps closer, then trails his fingertip down her arm. "But I do hope you play."

Kerrie's bright smile is tightening into a grimace, but the click of high heels on the marble floor thankfully draws Rollins' attention.

"Amy, darling. Come meet John and Lydia." He

turns back to us. "May I introduce my fiancée and your hostess?"

Fiancée?

Amy is tall and curvy and blonde, with eyes that are just a little too wide and a mouth that's a bit too small, making her appear meek and naive, an assessment I know to be false if her earlier interactions with Leo are any indication.

I notice that she does indeed wear an engagement ring, and she's twisting it nervously. This is a new development, and a potentially dangerous one. She might have been pressured into the engagement, making her even more of an asset as she'll want to ensure our help extricating her from Rollins. Or she may be so desperate to get away that she takes unnecessary risks.

Alternatively, she may have decided that she does love Rollins and that she doesn't want to betray him. I've seen it happen. A woman with scruples who loses them once she realizes the lifestyle she'll be landing in once he kicks her out.

I study Amy, trying to decide which side of that line she stands on, but I just can't get a read.

Meanwhile, Kerrie is playing the game the way it should be, gazing at the stone with a drippy expression and effusing, "Oh my gosh, that is beyond gorgeous. Have you set a date?"

"Soon," Amy says, and I hear the quiver in her voice. Amy must hear it, too, because her eyes widen with what I'm certain is fear.

"You must be so nervous," Kerrie says, once again stepping in and transforming an awkward, suspicious moment into stereotypical bridal jitters. "I mean, Johnny hasn't asked me—yet," she adds, with a Scarlett O'Hara smile in my direction. "But just knowing that I was going to be marrying such a powerful man? That must be a lot to process."

She beams at Rollins, looking at him as if he could walk on water, and undoubtedly feeding the man the kind of tripe his ego needs to thrive.

"Oh, it is," Amy agrees, her eyes going wide and her face painted with relief. "It's great to meet someone who gets it. Everyone just says how lucky I am, and I really am. But they don't understand the pressure of being married to a man like Michael. He's as sweet as pie, but I'm always afraid I won't live up to his expectations."

"Never," Rollins says, taking her hand and kissing it. "You're perfect, my sweet. How could you do anything but make me proud?"

Again, Amy's smile wavers, but I'm no longer

worried that Rollins will notice. This time, it just looks like she's overcome with emotion.

"Darling, I put them in the Magnolia Suite," Rollins says to her. "Would you mind showing them the way? Another guest has arrived and I should see to them."

"I'd be happy to," Amy says. "Magnolia is my favorite," she adds in a chipper hostess voice as we fall in step behind her.

As we walk, Amy chitters on about the house as if her head was full of soap bubbles. Maybe it is, but that would surprise me, because I saw a sharpness in her eyes.

The moment we enter the suite, Amy puts a finger to her lips. "The closet is over there," she says, pointing to a vase and then touching her ear. "And the bathroom is through those French doors." She indicates the television that sits on the dresser and surreptitiously taps her eyes.

Great. Audio and video surveillance. Isn't that just peachy? We brought countermeasures, of course, but I don't want to use them if the loss of signal will draw suspicion.

"Let me show you the tub," Amy says as we follow her once more. "The spigot's a little tricky, see?"

As she speaks, she easily turns on the water, then lowers her voice. "There's no surveillance in here. He tried, but the video would fog up and the water messed with the sound, so he eventually gave up."

I nod, and though I believe her, I'll still do a sweep after she leaves, just in case Rollins added bugs without telling her.

"Video in the TV and audio in the vase? Nothing else?" I want confirmation.

"That's it. And don't feel singled out. All the guests are bugged. Michael's not above blackmail. In fact, I think payouts are a pretty large percentage of his annual income."

"That fucker," Kerrie says, to which Amy just shrugs and nods.

"So tell me exactly what y'all need."

"Five minutes minimum at his computer. Fifteen is better in case someone is monitoring usage."

"That shouldn't be a problem. But I don't know his passwords."

I shake my head. "Don't worry about that. We've got it covered."

Her eyes go wide. "How?"

"If I understood that, I'd be in R&D and someone else would be here risking his neck."

In truth, I do understand it. Sort of. Okay, not

really. The way Noah described it, we're accomplishing the electronic equivalent of stealing the entire safe when all we're really after is the brick of gold inside. But we'll take the safe back home and crack it after we're free and clear. Only with a safe, the bad guy will notice that it's missing. With digital information, our larceny should go undetected.

That's the plan, anyway.

Hopefully it will work like Noah said. Not that I doubt him. The man's a genius, and now that he has billions of dollars in R&D money thanks to Damien Stark's worldwide conglomerate, he has the scratch to make the crazy things his brilliant mind conceives.

"So are we moving in tonight?"

I can tell by Kerrie's voice that she hopes so. Most of her nervousness is because of anticipation. Get the job over with and she can relax.

But Amy shakes her head. "He's always keyed up on the first night, making sure everyone's having a good time, that kind of thing. He'll notice if you wander. But he never stops drinking at these things. So by tomorrow, you could pop into Dallas and spend the day shopping and the odds are he wouldn't even blink."

"That works," I say. "Plus it gives me time to get

a feel for his patterns. Will you be able to get away from him to go with me?" I ask Amy.

"I don't think that will be a problem at all. He likes to say we're exclusive except when we're not." She smiles at Kerrie. "And I'm sure he'll be more than happy keeping you company."

"Great," Kerrie says.

I think about the man and the way he leered at her. And I know right then that as simple as this assignment may look on paper, it's still going to rank as the hardest in my career.

CHAPTER NINE

YES, I know that the plan was for Kerrie to cozy up to Rollins so that Amy and I could get away.

And yes, I know what's riding on the plan working out.

Moreover, I know that Kerrie is perfectly capable of taking care of herself with that arrogant fucktard of a human.

I know all of that; I do.

And at the same time when I see the way Rollins' hand slides over her ass as he moves behind her, I pretty much want to rip his balls off. The man's dangerous, after all. And the thought of him touching her makes me ill.

At the same time, I can't really blame him for being so handsy. Kerrie looks incredible.

We'd been unsure about the dress code, a problem that I solved by bringing jeans and a Henley as one option and a tailored silk suit as the other.

To this, Kerrie informed me that I was not only cheating, but that as a man I didn't realize how difficult it is to maneuver in her world. When she unpacked in our room, I understood what she meant. Being careful to remain in character as Lydia and John, she showed me the options she'd brought. A tube style gown you might see on a hooker trolling for tricks in Hollywood. A denim miniskirt and a midriff-revealing top that accentuated her assets in a way that I thoroughly approved of, but which didn't come under the umbrella of elegant. A sexy cocktail dress that I thought would be just fine, but that she insisted was too "pearls and snobbery."

"I have a few other things, too," she said. "But nothing that feels right."

I just stood there in my suit and thanked my parents for providing me with my particular pair of chromosomes.

Finally, she remembered that there were outfits in the closet. And that's where she found the shimmery gold gown with the plunging back, equally revealing neckline, and a slit up her left thigh that made no allowance for underwear.

She's wearing it now and looks good enough to eat, and from the stares she's getting from both men and women as they mingle in the ballroom, I know that I'm not the only one who thinks so.

The material has some stretch to it, and it clings to the curve of her ass, which is where Rollins' hand dallies before sliding over a bit so that his fingertips caress the bare skin of her thigh.

She turns, ostensibly to talk to him more directly, but it has the effect of shifting his hand away from her bare thigh and back to her ass. Under the circumstances, I consider that an improvement.

At least I do until his fingers creep up. And when I see him brush the pad of his thumb on the skin at the base of her spine, I realize I have to intervene. Not for me, but for her. She's going to have to deal with him all alone tomorrow when Amy and I make our escape. Tonight, she deserves to relax with me.

A waiter glides by with a tray of champagne, and I grab two glasses, then join them. "Lydia," I say, handing her a flute, then sliding my free hand around her waist as I nod to Rollins, claiming what's mine.

She turns to me, and I see the trust—and the gratitude—in her eyes. I want to pull her close and kiss her. And since Rollins is watching us—and since it's that kind of party—that's exactly what I do.

She's just sipped her champagne, and I can still taste the tingle of tiny bubbles on her lips. She gasps in surprise, but doesn't pull away, instead she deepens the kiss, her body going soft in my arms, her mouth opening to me. I close my eyes, wishing we were anywhere but here and at the same time grateful that this is exactly where we are, because under what other circumstances would I have done this?

I know better, after all. I know exactly what kind of door I'm opening.

And I know damn well that once this fantasy of John and Lydia is over, I'm going to have to close it tight again.

I pull away gently, breaking the kiss. Her lips are parted, her skin flushed, and her nipples are hard against the soft, clingy material. I take a step back, sucking in air to get my own body under control. Because right now, all I can think about is ripping that dress off of her and tasting every delicious inch of her sweet little body.

I meet Rollins' eyes and note the way he's watching us, his own face flush with desire. "I think

Lydia and I are going to go explore. There must be a dark corner around here somewhere."

The corner of his mouth quirks up, and I'm quite certain that his eyes are following us. If I were to take her into a dark corner and do all the things I want, I'm absolutely positive that Rollins would follow.

"Thank you," she whispers as we move away.

"For the kiss?"

"Yes." Her smile teases me. "And for rescuing me. At least until tomorrow. Tomorrow, I guess there's no rescue allowed." She sighs, and I have to join in. Because she's right.

Great.

"Then again, maybe it won't be so bad." She glances around the room. "Considering this is supposed to be a sex party, it seems rather tame. Maybe all he'll want to do tomorrow is play chess."

"I wouldn't count on that. But you're right about the party."

I look around, too. There are couples and clusters everywhere. Amy told us the house has twenty bedrooms and all are occupied by two people at a minimum. There are also a dozen or so people staying in a guest-house about half a mile away on the property. So the place is teeming. But it's not like we're in a porn film. Hell, it's not even like we're at a Vegas strip club.

"I'd conjured up a lot more risqué things in my imagination," she says.

"Oh, really?" We're in the dining room now, standing in a corner near the food-laden table.

She takes a step toward me, then cups her hands on my ass as she eases against me. I watch as she bites her lower lip, and I know that she can tell exactly what kind of effect the feel of her is having on me.

"Lydia..."

The corner of her mouth twitches. "Hmm?"

But I say nothing. Instead, my hand glides around to trace the plunging edge of her dress, my fingertip warm against her soft skin. I watch as she closes her eyes, as her breath comes in short, stuttering gasps. Her teeth drag across her lower lip, and she opens her eyes, soft with a desire so familiar to me it makes my heart ache.

"John." She swallows. "Please."

"Please what?" I want to hear it. I want her to beg for my touch. I want to close my eyes and imagine all of our nights, remembering the feel of her in my arms, the joy of knowing that this incredible woman belonged to me.

"Please don't start something you're not willing

to finish."

Crash!

And just like that, the moment shatters. Because what the hell am I doing? Where am I taking this? How can I justify this moment—or where this moment was going—knowing that it can't go anywhere?

I take a step back. "I'm sorry."

She licks her lips, then nods. "Yeah. Me, too."

I take her hand. "Come on." This time, I lead her outside. The backyard is like a fairy land with twinkling lights, intimate seating areas, a steaming hot tub, a crystal clear pool, and walking paths through the kind of garden that usually isn't found on North Texas ranch land. Presumably, Rollins pays a fortune for irrigation and landscaping.

"Should we sue for false advertising?"

I shoot her a questioning glance.

"The party. Not really as expected."

"Disappointed?"

I'm teasing, but she considers the question. "I'll admit to being curious. But if a bunch of people standing around talking while a few more make out in corners constitutes a sex party, then I went to at least half a dozen my senior year of high school."

I chuckle. "Guess I've been to quite a few sex

parties myself if that's the definition."

I love the way she laughs. None of that ridiculous attempt to pull back. When she finds something amusing, she doesn't try to hide it. With Kerrie, what you see is what you get, and I've always admired the hell out of her for that.

Casually, she reaches over and takes my hand. I glance down, more affected by her touch than I want to let on.

"I want to talk to you. It's easier if I'm holding your hand."

My chest constricts with apprehension, but I simply nod. "All right."

"I just want to say that I get it. Why we broke up, I mean."

I turn just enough to see her face, trying to ascertain where she's going with this.

"I don't agree with it," she adds, with enough humor in her voice that I know she's not looking for an argument, "but I do understand."

She pauses, as if making sure that *I* understand. So I nod and say, "I'm glad to hear it."

"And I really do want to stay friends."

"So do I. If you're still worried about what I said in the office—about that not being possible, I mean—I was just—"

"No, no, I get it. I cornered you and it was weird and we're fine." She draws a breath. "But you are right that it can be awkward. And I don't want things to be awkward between us."

"Oh, Ke-Lydia." I wince, then watch her fight not to laugh. It's not as if we think that there's surveillance out here. I'm actually pretty sure there's not, as I have a bug detector in my pocket. Any mics, and it should be vibrating. But I also don't want to drop character too much. "I don't want that either," I assure her.

She draws a breath. "That's why I'm thinking about taking another job."

We've been walking through a young maze, not too tricky since the hedge is only about shoulder height. Now, I pull her to a stop. "What are you talking about? What job?"

She starts to rub her chin with her thumb, something she does only when she's nervous.

"Lydia..."

"I'm thinking of moving to Los Angeles, okay?"

The words hit me with the force of a wrecking ball, and I take a step back, stunned. "What? Why?"

"Delilah asked me to come work for her. Like a manager, but not. I'd basically help run her life. All the stuff that a star needs except for the actual

Hollywood part, which I know nothing about. But her finances and organizing her life and arranging her travel and overseeing security and on and on."

I stand there in shock. "Does Pierce know about this?" Delilah is Pierce's sister-in-law. He and Jezebel met when Delilah, a young movie star, was in town and needed protection from some truly rabid fans.

"Not yet. I was talking to Del about us, and one thing led to another. I'm seriously considering the job. The title is executive assistant, and the woman who did have the job recently married and moved to Chicago."

"You're really thinking about leaving?"

Her shoulders rise and fall. "I'd miss you. But the thing is, I already miss you, you know? And I do think that we can go back to the way things were before the utility room. But I also know that in the back of my mind, I'm always going to be wondering if history will repeat itself. And the real kicker—the thing that lets me know that leaving is right—is that I want it to."

"I don't know what to say," I admit. I can't tell her I want that as well. It was my decision to break up, and I know it was the right one. I have to at least give the illusion of being strong.

"Age really is just a number, you know."

"We've had this conversation. You know my reasons. We both know I'm right."

She shakes her head. "No, I don't know that at all. In fact, I think you're dead wrong. You're grandmother loved your grandfather. It wasn't an imposition when his health declined. And your mother was an idiot. I'm not an idiot. And just because you're older doesn't mean you're going to get old and feeble before me. And just because you were in combat and exposed to all sorts of weird shit doesn't mean you're going to fall down dead tomorrow."

She sucks in air. "I get it. I do. But don't put words in my mouth. I think you're wrong. Hell, I'm certain you're wrong. But that doesn't matter. Because while couples can have disagreements, whether or not to be together can't be a subject that's up for debate. So I respect your decision. I do. And I want to be your friend. Truly. But I just think that it will be easier from fifteen hundred miles away."

I swallow. Then nod. Then slide my hands into my pockets. "I get it."

"Do you?"

"Same as you. I don't like it. But I get it."

She flashes me a wide, side smile. "See? We really are compatible."

Despite myself, I laugh.

"I didn't mean to lay all of this on you, tonight. I mean, if there was any sort of bondage or wild fondling going on in there, I never would have brought it up."

At that, we both laugh. We also decide that we've escaped the party long enough, and so we head back to the sex party that lacks sex, only to find out that we made our assessment far too early. Because as soon as we enter the house, it's clear that things have changed.

The lights are off, and now the interior is illuminated only by candlelight, the orange light flickering over bare flesh. It's as if our departure was everyone's cue to get busy. From where we stand in the kitchen, we can see that there are couples and threesomes and foursomes on sofas and on the floor of the room beyond. And just a few feet away, a woman on her knees is giving a blowjob to a man leaning back against the counter. To our left, in the dining room, a woman is strapped naked and spread-eagled to the table as another woman brushes the soft end of a flail over her body, then snaps it, making the woman cry out in a mixture of pain and bliss.

"Oh," Kerrie says, and for a second I think that's a reaction to what we're seeing. Then I realize that she's seen Rollins. He's heading toward us, though I don't think he's seen us yet. Nor do I want him to. She's going to be with him—in this environment— tomorrow. As far as I'm concerned, that's more time with her than he deserves.

I tug her sideways until we end up in a narrow butler's pantry. I put my finger over her lips, and she nods. We can't see him now, but I can hear someone walking. I can also hear the sounds of sex all around us.

"Does it turn you on?" I whisper, then immediately regret my words.

She meets my eyes. "Yes. And no."

I wait, silently inviting her to explain. For a moment, we just look at each other. Then she steps forward, her arms sliding around my neck, her mouth brushing my ear as she speaks.

"It's hot, like when we'd watch porn. Remember?"

I do, and the feel of her lips and the whisper of breath are as arousing as her words.

"But I never wanted to be in the movie, and I don't want to be on display here. Public group sex isn't my thing. I just wanted—I *want*—to be with you." She runs her tongue along the edge of my ear, and I stifle a moan.

I should put a stop to this. Weren't we just having the friends-only talk? "We shouldn't," I manage.

"Probably not. But I'm leaving anyway. The utility room was hardly a good send off. There's a bedroom here. And a shower with jets."

Her hand slides down to stroke me. I'm already as hard as steel. "What about Leo?"

Her hand stills. "Huh?"

"Aren't you two seeing each other?"

Again, her tongue teases me. "Would that be a problem?"

"Hell, yes."

Her laugh is like the tinkling of bells. "We're not dating. What gave you that idea?"

I don't bother answering. They're friends, of course. And I wished a relationship on her because I want her happy. Because I didn't want to be the asshole who loved her and left her.

Still...

"We shouldn't. You know we shouldn't."

But she just shakes her head. "No, John, you're wrong. It's a sex party, remember? And we're not Kerrie and Connor," she adds, her voice so soft I can barely hear it, even with her lips against my ear. "We're Lydia and John. And they're hot and heavy.

So isn't that what we need to be? Isn't that how to not only survive undercover, but to excel at it? To get fully and completely into character? To embrace the role?"

She slides around my body until her ass is pressed against me. "So let's embrace it." She takes my hand and rests it on her thigh. Then she takes my other hand and cups it over her breast. And God help me I let her. For that matter, it's all I can do not to yank her skirt up and fuck her right there. Hell, it's private enough.

And when she eases her hand onto mine, then starts to inch our way up her thigh, I know that whatever battle I've been fighting is a lost cause. I take control, easing my fingers up, teasing the soft skin between her thigh and her pussy, and then slowly—so deliciously slowly—teasing my finger along her slit, reveling in how damn wet she is for me.

"John?" Her voice is rough. Needy.

"Yes?"

"Now," she demands. "Please, please fuck me now."

CHAPTER TEN

THAT IS an invitation I'm not prepared to ignore, especially when her low, sensual groan entices me as I ease my finger inside her, my cock now painfully hard.

"God, yes," she murmurs, her hips moving as I finger fuck her fast and deep. "More," she demands. "Con—*John*. Please. Please, I want more. I want everything. *You*," she says, making my heart swell. "I want you."

"Upstairs," I say, but she shakes her head. "Now. Here." It's a demand, and oh, Christ, how the hell do I say no to that? "Are there doors?"

I glance to both sides. "No." Apparently it's not a butler's pantry after all. More like a damn butler's hallway, and I don't care what kind of party we're at, I can't fuck her here where anyone can walk in, anyone can see. I'm not that guy.

But at the same time, who am I to ignore her demands. Maybe I can't fuck her, but I can make her come. *That* I want to do. To hold her here in the dark in her slinky gold dress. To play my fingers over her clit. To listen as her sensual sounds join the moans and sighs filling the air around us.

Yeah, I'm all over that.

"Just relax, baby," I whisper, as I tease her clit, stroking and playing with her pussy as my other hand slides inside that low-cut dress to find her nipple and squeeze it hard between my thumb and forefinger.

I know Kerrie's body as well as I know my own, and I can tell that she's already close. Her nipple is tight under my fingers, her breasts full and heavy. And her core is slick and hot, her clit hard and sensitive.

Usually, she's a slow build, and I'll take my time, playing and teasing and coaxing an explosive orgasm out of her. But now I'm thinking that she likes the hint of danger. The possibility that we're being watched. Because I can tell how turned on she is, how much this whole kinky scenario has revved her up. And damned if it doesn't make me even harder.

So, yeah. I want to fuck her. Want to sink myself deep inside her. But not here. And not yet.

Right now, this is all about her.

Her hips move in the kind of rhythm that lets me know that what I'm doing is exactly what she wants, and damned if the whole scene isn't erotic as hell. Me getting her off, her on the knife-edge of what promises to be an explosive orgasm, and the sounds of sex all around us.

"That's it, baby. Come for me," I order. "Explode for me, so I can take you upstairs and fuck you all over again."

She moans, then reaches up, cupping her hand over mine and forcing me to squeeze her breast harder as she arches back, her entire body shaking as she goes completely over the edge, her core tightening so hard around my fingers I fear for my circulation.

She grinds against my hand, her body on overdrive, as I continue thrusting, wanting to keep her on edge as her climax explodes in wave after delicious wave that almost sends me over as well, until finally her legs sag and she starts to sink, her little body utterly worn out.

I catch her as she goes down, scooping her up and holding her close as she hooks her arms around my neck. "That was incredible." Her voice caresses me, the sound like liquid sex.

"It really was," I agree. "Want more?"

Her laugh delights me. "I want you to take me to our room and fuck me so deep they can hear me scream all the way down here."

Considering how hard her words make me, I think that may actually be possible. Assuming I can get us to the room. Carrying her and walking with my cock this hard is no easy task. But I wasn't a soldier for nothing, and soon enough we reach the room.

I gently put her on the bed, then turn on the music in defense against the microphone. I'm tempted to let whoever's tuned in get a thrill by listening to us, but I figure they probably get enough of that. Plus, I don't want them to hear our real names if one of us makes a mistake in bed.

As for the television, I'm not sure about that. The one thing I know for certain is that I have no interest in starring in a sex tape. There's always the bathroom, but I've never been one for making love in a whirlpool tub. Call me old fashioned, but I like a bed.

I can tell that Kerrie is thinking along the same lines, and after a moment, she sits up, then slides off the bed. Then she indicates that she wants me to sit.

"Showtime," she says, taking my phone off the dresser and scrolling through the streaming app until she finds a playlist of sexy, sultry songs.

I watch, mesmerized, as she dances in front of me, her hands going to the side zipper of her dress. She wriggles her hips and shoulders and the entire garment slithers down, leaving her completely naked.

Whoever's at the other end of that video feed is getting quite a show, but since I know Kerrie's aware of that, too, I don't say a word. Instead, I watch as she bends over, picks up the dress, then tosses it over the television, taking care to cover the top middle where the camera would be embedded. "I'll hang it up later," she says loudly, obviously for the benefit of our undoubtedly disappointed audience. "Right now, I just want you."

Then she turns up the volume on the speaker, tosses my phone onto a nearby chair, and moves to stand in front of me.

"Okay?" She asks, and she pushes me back, then climbs onto the bed. Now I'm leaning back on my elbows, still fully clothed, and she's riding me, her hot little body enticing me, and her slick core leaving a wet patch on the silk blend of my pants where she's rubbing herself against my thigh.

It's ridiculously sexy, and part of me wants to stay like that, watching her use my body to get herself off. But it's just not enough, and when I can't take it anymore, I grab her waist, flip her onto her back, and close my mouth over hers.

I kiss her long and deep, and she responds with wild enthusiasm, arms and legs clutching me tight, pulling me to her. "Too many clothes," she murmurs. "I want you naked."

That's easy enough to remedy, and soon my clothes are on the floor, my skin warm against hers. "Please," she begs. "I don't want to go slow. I just want you inside me."

"Oh, baby." I meet her eyes, looking deep. This is more than just the eroticism of the weekend. It's more than play-acting Lydia and John. This is the desire that has always burned between us. A desire I know well. That I wish we could nurture. But we both know that this weekend is going to be the end. Our last hurrah.

And dammit, we're going to make the most of it.

I lower my mouth to hers, wanting the kiss to start slowly. But I'm too aroused, too lost in the scent and taste of her. Instead of slow and sensual, our mouths clash violently, a wild kiss. A claiming. A demand.

We devour each other, and then I move down, tasting her neck, teasing her collar bone, sucking on her sensitive breasts as she arches up, squirming beneath me, taking more and more until she twines her fingers in my hair and urges me down lower.

I go eagerly, wanting the taste of her. Wanting to tease her all the way to the edge with my tongue. She's soft and sweet and she moves against me in a way that always takes me to the brink. There's no question with Kerrie that she likes what I'm doing. With her, sex is an all-in proposition; something that I've always found so damned arousing.

"Yes," she cries as I suck on her swollen clit, her hips bucking with passion as another orgasm washes over her and she grinds against my mouth, riding it out until she's gasping and begging for more. Begging for me to thrust deep inside of her.

"Hard," she begs. "Fast."

And that's what I give her. Thrusting in deep and riding her, our bodies slamming together in a wild frenzy until I clench up, frozen for that sweet moment before I explode, filling her, and then collapsing, spent, on top of her.

She strokes my hair, sighing with contentment. "That was incredible," she says. And then, even though I've barely had time to catch my breath, she asks sweetly, "Can we do it again?"

And, honestly, how the hell can I say no to that?

CHAPTER ELEVEN

I WAKE to the familiar feel of Kerrie beside me, her naked body pressed against mine, her leg thrown over me as if to keep me beside her. She's a possessive sleeper, and I used to revel in that, knowing that even deep in sleep she wanted to be near me.

I feel no different now, and I pull her close, breathing in the fresh scent of her hair and the musky smell of sex that lingers on our bodies and the sheets. Today's the day, and I don't want to let her go. Because what if something goes wrong and Rollins realizes our game? What if she gets caught or hurt or worse? How the hell could I live with myself?

You broke her heart. You're living with that.

I push the thought away. She understands. And she's doing fine.

She's leaving. Moving away from her family and friends because of you.

"Del is family," I mutter, only realizing I've spoken aloud when she stirs.

"Did you say something?"

"I said good morning," I lie, then kiss her, glowing with warmth when she rolls over so that she can wrap her arms around me.

"Can we just stay here all day?"

"I can't think of anything I'd like better," I admit.

"But?"

I laugh. "But if we did that, I couldn't make love to you in the shower."

She studies my face, then props herself up on her elbow. "I need some music to help me wake up." She grabs my phone off the windowsill above us. Then she opens a music app, connects my speaker to Bluetooth, and blares the music just loud enough to ensure we can talk in privacy.

"I thought last night was a one off." She's whispering, but I can hear the note of eagerness in her voice.

"Did you want it to be?"

I see her throat move as she swallows. "You know

what I want." She meets my eyes, her gaze steady. "I've wanted it since the first day Pierce dragged your sorry ass home with him when you guys were on leave."

"And you know I can't offer that."

She nods. "I know. I do. If memory serves, I was the one who convinced you that last night would be a good idea. And I was right, wasn't I?"

"Last night was incredible."

She nods firmly. "Okay."

"Okay, what?"

"Last night wasn't a one-off, but it also wasn't a beginning. It was the Lydia and John show. A limited run. No touring production. Call it a bubble or an anomaly, it doesn't matter. Hell, we can call it a glorious send-off, because once we get back, I really am giving notice. I can't do this with you and stay. I wish I could be that girl—I thought I could. Before the utility room, I think I even was. There was a dull ache when I was around you, but I handled it. I don't think I can handle it any more."

I nod. I know exactly what she means.

"So John and Lydia?" Her voice rises in question.

"Is that a yes?" I think it is, but I want to be absolutely clear that we're on the same page.

Her smile is wide and a little bit devious. "It's

not only a yes, it's a hell yes. Because if this is our last run, *John*, I want to go out wild. I want everything. And then I'm going to store it in my heart, a dirty sweet memory that I can pull out whenever I need to. Deal?"

I slide out of bed and stand up, my hand held out to her. "Deal," I say. "Now let's go make it official with a fast fuck in the shower."

She laughs as I pull her to her feet. "I'll say one thing. You sure do know how to romance a girl."

———

If last night's atmosphere could be described as darkly raunchy, today's is steamy and sticky.

The Texas sun beats down on the back yard, and dozens of naked men and women sprawl on the cushioned chaises that surround the huge, rectangular pool.

Another dozen or so float or swim in the water. And a few rebellious types even wear bathing suits.

One couple is fucking languorously under a giant umbrella, the woman's loud moans acting as a counterpoint to the wet smack of the volleyball that two well-endowed women are batting back and forth over a net.

It's all very surreal and not my scene at all. Though I can't deny that I'm enjoying stealing glances at Kerrie beside me. She's topless, but she drew the line at removing her bikini bottoms. A decision I heartily approve of. I'm not the sharing type.

Unlike last night, which apparently got even wilder after Kerrie and I moved our private party to our room, today feels like we've time traveled to the sixties and stumbled upon a nudist commune.

Tamer, but still not my scene. And while I can't deny that fucking Kerrie in the butler's pantry was seriously hot, this assignment has driven home that public sex and sex parties aren't my thing at all.

On the contrary, I'm a one-woman man, and I don't like to share.

For a moment, I let myself acknowledge that the *one woman* in that equation is Kerrie. But that's false reasoning. The one woman *in this moment* is Kerrie. And I just need to keep reminding myself of that.

This weekend, that woman is Kerrie.

Right now, that woman is Kerrie.

But moving forward? That's a different story altogether.

I glance over at the woman beside me, soaking up the sun. She's lithe and lovely, and I'm not the only one who thinks so. That much I can tell by the attention she's drawing from everyone who passes in front of the area we've staked out.

Kerrie, of course, notices none of it, as her eyes are not only closed, but covered with cucumber slices. She's been that way for the last fifteen minutes, and I'm under strict orders to wake her at thirty so that she can turn over. "Especially since my tits aren't used to the sun," she'd added.

When I asked why she didn't keep her top on if she was worried, she shrugged. "When in Rome. Besides, who wants tan lines if you can avoid them? And what's the big deal anyway? They're just breasts."

I almost countered that I was feeling proprietary about them and didn't want to share with the entire party. But considering the limitations of our weekend arrangement, I decided I didn't have the right.

As I study her now, I notice Rollins heading our way. "I didn't see much of you two last night," he says as he pauses beside Kerrie's lounge chair.

"We had our own private party," I confess, since with the surveillance in our room, he must know that anyway. "You might say the atmosphere downstairs inspired us."

"In that case I won't be insulted. But now that you've got that out of your system, I expect we'll see you downstairs tonight." His gaze cuts to Kerrie. "I want to claim my dance with Lydia. And anything else I can persuade you to give me." His words are directed to me but his gaze is on Kerrie as she sits up, peeling the cucumbers off her eyes.

She smiles at him, not self-conscious at all as he stares at her breasts.

"She'll need to be in on that negotiation," I say. "Unlike some of your guests, I can't claim ownership of the woman I'm with."

She turns a wide, genuine smile on me before returning her attention to Rollins. "Well, you know that Johnny has my heart. But I suppose there are parts of me that are available for sharing. The three of us could make some sort of deal, don't you think, darling?"

"I do," I say, deliberately looking toward Amy, who's standing by the bar chatting with the bartender.

Rollins follows my gaze, then chuckles. "Oh, yes. That can definitely be arranged."

"You can speak for her?" Kerrie asks innocently.

"Of course," he says, then tilts his head in

dismissal before continuing down the path, chatting with the other guests sunbathing by the pool.

I meet Kerrie's eyes, and it's clear that we're both fighting the urge to laugh. "Come on," I say. "Let's go get cleaned up before cocktails."

"I've got a better idea," she says, falling in step beside me as she pulls on a T-shirt. "Why don't we go up to the room, get dirty, and *then* get cleaned up?"

"Dirty, huh?"

She grins, and I laugh.

"Aren't you a sexy little sinner?"

"Absolutely," she says. "And you know you like it."

CHAPTER TWELVE

THERE'S a lot to be said for lazy, afternoon sex, and I'm feeling relaxed and highly confident about tonight's mission when we finally roll out of bed to shower and dress for both tonight's party and tonight's adventure.

"So we're clear, right?" I ask, after cranking up the volume on our music. "You'll be his charming little sidepiece, and Amy and I will head to the study. I can't imagine he'll follow but if he does, text me the moment he steps away from you."

"Will do. And if he insists I come with him, I'll pretend I'm checking a text from my sister. I'll text you a heart emoji, so that if he sees it, I can say I was just telling you how much I missed you."

I nod. "Perfect."

As we talk, I've been taking the device out of its small case. Barely bigger than a business card, the gizmo hooks into a computer by port or Bluetooth. We'll be using a port, and I have the adaptor already attached to the tiny thing.

Once attached, it goes in and essentially downloads the computer's equivalent of DNA. Then its counterpart at Noah's office takes that data, applies a billion to the nth byte of processing power, and does a Watson and Crick number on the information, unraveling that computer DNA strand so that it can then rebuild the guts of the information. How it does that without requiring a password, I have no idea. But Noah assures me it will.

All of which means that if Carrington-Kohl's proprietary information is in there, we'll know Rollins' people stole it, and Brody Carrington can decide what his next move is.

"Hard to believe it's so simple," she says after I've run through all of that.

I don't disagree. But since it's backed by both Noah and the Stark name, I'm confident it's going to work.

I skim my eyes over her outfit, another low-cut

number that accentuates her cleavage and her ass. "And you? How's your confidence level?"

"I can handle it," she says. "I can't say I'm looking forward to being touched by that man, but I can take one for the team. I just hope he doesn't expect..."

She trails off with a shudder, and I don't blame her.

"He can expect whatever he wants," I say. "But that doesn't mean he gets. You have your secret weapon?"

She grins and nods, then reaches into her cleavage and extracts the tiny bottle she's tucked into the hidden pocket. It's Ipecac syrup, and it's a last resort in case she needs to escape. Because Ipecac induces vomiting, and surely that will destroy even a man like Rollins' amorous edge.

"Good," I say. "Don't hesitate to use it if he pushes too hard."

"Believe me. I won't."

I watch as she takes a deep breath, then nods. "Ready," she says, and we head down to join the party.

Tonight, things have heated up earlier than before. It's the last night, after all, and I assume everyone wants to indulge as much as possible. That's fine with me. It means the liquor's been flowing for hours, and everyone—Rollins included—is already well lubricated. That can only help our mission.

When we see Rollins, though, my stomach twists into knots. He practically licks his lips as he stares at her tits. And when he follows that class act up with, "Oh, yes, my dear. You're definitely the cherry on tonight's sundae," I consider calling abort and getting the hell out of there.

Kerrie, however, is completely professional. She sidles up to him, smiles, and says, well if you've got me, where's Amy for John?"

Immediately, he signals for her, and she hurries over, looking both submissive and annoyed, which is exactly what we'd rehearsed. "You're with John tonight, baby," he says, then turns away in dismissal before she even acknowledges his words.

I meet Amy's eyes, see the flare of anger, and any lingering doubt as to her loyalty to me and Kerrie flies out the window. She takes my hand, then coos, "I know just the place for us," before leading me toward a back service hall where I happen to know Rollins' private office is hidden in a high-security room to which Amy has full access.

Maybe that's Rollins' one redeeming quality—he trusts the women he takes into his bed.

I glance back to make sure Rollins isn't paying attention to us before we duck into the hall. He's not. How could he be? Every ounce of his attention is focused on Kerrie, including the hand that's slowly creeping up her thigh. She's sitting rigid, and I know she hates this. She wants to nail him, and she's making the sacrifice for the good of our operation, but she hates it.

So do I. Because how can I do this to a woman I love?

Love. Yeah, there's that word. And it's true. I do love her. But where the two of us are concerned, I don't know what that means in the larger context. All I know is that right here, right now, it means that I can't let her go through with this.

There has to be another way.

"Change of plans," I say to Amy, who eyes me as if I'm crazy while I lay out the revised approach. Hell, I probably am.

Moments later, Kerrie gapes at me as I hurry across the room, but her stare isn't as bold and confused as Rollins'. He, however, recovers quickly. "Problem?" he asks.

"More like a proposition." Amy's caught up

with me, and I meet Kerrie's eyes, then scratch my chest, right about where the Ipecac would be if I were her.

For a moment she looks confused, but when I turn my attention to Rollins, I realize she gets it. I'm afraid she's going to argue, but she has to know I have a new plan. I'm not going to sacrifice the mission. I'm just going to save her.

Thankfully, that reality must dawn on her. Because as I start to talk, she surreptitiously takes out the small bottle, opens it, and quickly swallows the contents.

Meanwhile, I've moved behind Amy so that my hands are on her breasts. "We want to watch," I say, amused when Kerrie's eyes go wide with shock. But it's not shock on Rollins' face. It's excitement.

"Do you?"

I trace Amy's lower lip with my fingertip until she starts to suck, playing the role we'd quickly discussed. Beside Rollins, I see Kerrie start to retch.

Rollins hasn't noticed. He's too intrigued by my proposition. "I like the way you think, Mr. London. Perhaps we should—"

But I don't know what he was going to suggest, because that's when Kerrie vomits all over his fine Oriental carpet.

"I'm so sorry," she says. "I don't usually drink, and—"

"It's okay, honey," Amy says, sliding into maternal mode and helping Kerrie to her feet. Let's go get you cleaned up."

The women escape before Rollins manages to gather himself. I study his face, looking for signs that he saw through the charade or that he's going to take out his frustration on Amy later. But all he does is look at me soberly and say, "Well, if watching is your kink, let's see who else I can find so we can get you off good and proper."

Does this guy have his host duties down pat, or what?

He heads out, leaving me alone for a good half hour as he presumably searches out a companion. Fortunately, before he finds the lucky woman to pair with him for my entertainment, Amy returns. I relax immediately, understanding that the girls were able to run the tap and gather the computer DNA.

"I tucked her into bed," she says as Rollins returns with a tall, thin blonde. "She's got a little bit of a fever, so I don't think it's alcohol. She really wants you with her."

I try to look disappointed. "I'll be back once she

falls asleep," I lie. Then I nod to Amy and head upstairs, my body practically dripping with relief.

I don't relax until I get into the room, though. The music is playing and there's a robe over the television. I want to cry out with joy at our success. I want her to tell me exactly how it went down, and from the way her eyes are shining, I know she wants to tell me, too.

Mostly, though I want to pull her close and fuck her until she explodes with long, passionate cries.

But she's sick, or she's supposed to be. Which means we can't have whoever is monitoring the mics and cameras wondering why the sick girl is suddenly having wild sex.

That's okay, though, I think as I strip and climb into bed with her. "You did great," I whisper. "How's your stomach?"

"Getting better."

"Yeah? I should check." I slide back the covers and see that she's wearing only a tank top and tiny panties. I lift up the tank and press a kiss to her belly. "Better?"

She doesn't actually answer, but I interpret her soft moan of pleasure as a yes.

I lift my head and meet her eyes. "You were amazing," I say.

"I would have stayed with him," she whispers, then tangles her fingers in my hair. "But I would have hated it. Thank you so much for rescuing me."

"I couldn't stand the thought of him touching you," I say. "That's my job. For this weekend at least, I'm the only one who has that privilege."

"In that case," she says, "quit talking and start touching."

I eagerly do as ordered, pulling her roughly to me and closing my mouth over hers. She tastes like sin and strawberries, and I could kiss her all night. Enjoying the softness of her lips, the wild exploration of her tongue against mine. The way our passion ramps up as our kisses mimic sex, growing in need and desire. In wildness and heat.

Soon, though, it's not enough. I need more. I need all of her. I need to claim her. To have her. I suck on her breast through the tank as my fingers slip down under her panties. She's hot and slick, and I want more than my fingers inside her. I want all of her. All of us.

Gently, I peel off her panties, but leave on the tank. We still have to be quiet—just in case—but right now I can't turn back. I have to be inside her.

I meet her eyes, see the way she bites her lower lip, and know that I can't wait any longer. I ease between her legs, taking it slow and easy, going deeper with each thrust, biting back my own moans of pleasure and covering her mouth when she forgets and starts to cry out.

Our eyes meet, and I see the humor there. And that moment is everything to me. Because this is *us*, not just sex. It's friendship and fun and heat and lust, and that drives me harder and harder, until we're staring into each others eyes, both of us right on the edge.

Then her body tightens around me, and as she bites her lip to keep from crying out, she pulls me over the edge with her, and we tumble off into space together

It's magic, I think. This thing between us. This intensity. This attraction. This need. Magic, pure and simple.

But the real trick is going to be surviving once we get out into the real world again. Once we walk away from what we've rebuilt, and everything we've shared between us this weekend disappears into the mist of memory.

CHAPTER THIRTEEN

WHEN WE RETURN to Austin on Sunday afternoon, we're greeted with much praise and applause, the bulk of which is aimed at Kerrie in congratulations of her first real undercover operation.

"Modeling doesn't count," Gracie tells her, leaning against Cayden as we all gather in Pierce and Jezebel's backyard garden. "You're such a natural, it was hardly a stretch. And I wasn't evil." A stunning woman, Gracie has made a successful career as a plus-size model.

"Maybe a little evil," Cayden teases, making Gracie roll her eyes.

"Who's evil?" Jez asks, joining us with a tray of coffee, wine, cookies, and cheese. "Did Noah call?

Did we catch Rollins?" The weekend get together is part of our regular routine, but today is slightly different as we're waiting to hear back from Noah, with whom we left the device on our way in from town.

"Oh, he's evil," Pierce tells her. "We just don't have the proof yet." He glances at his watch, then frowns. "It's only been a few hours."

Kerrie shrugs as she takes a glass of wine, passing me one, too. I bite back a smile; she knows me well. After our adventure, this just isn't a coffee kind of afternoon. "When we dropped it off with him," she says, "Noah told us it could be fast or it might take until tomorrow. Or longer." She lifts a shoulder. "Lots of factors, I guess."

"It's all good," Leo says. "Gives us more time to just enjoy hanging out, and to celebrate Connor and Kerrie's safe return from the jaws of hell." This is his first weekend to chill with us, and when he casually grabs a cookie from the tray, I know he'll fit right in.

"So how was it?" Jez asks. Glancing sideways toward Pierce. "I've never been to a sex party."

"Nonsense," he scoffs. "We host private parties pretty much nightly."

Jez shoots him a scowl, but I can tell she's fighting a smile.

"You didn't run across that kind of thing in Hollywood?" Kerrie asks, which makes the jealous green monsters in my belly start hopping. Is *that* what she'll get up to when she moves west to work with Del?

Jez's brows rise. "With my sister's schedule? Who had time for that? Not that I was ever invited. Or would go. But no. No invitations. No hints. And no regrets."

"Good," Pierce says, kissing her forehead.

"I've heard of them in the modeling world," Gracie puts in. "Not really my thing."

Cayden releases an exaggerated sigh. "Damn," he says, earning him a shove from his wife-to-be.

We all look to Leo, who holds up his hands and shakes his head. "I take the Fifth," he says, but I can't tell whether he's being serious or pulling our legs.

Soon enough, we shift gears, moving off the topic of work to general weekend chatter. As Pierce tells me about their new sprinkler system—and I remind myself why I prefer condo living—I can't help but notice that Kerrie and Leo are sitting on the glider, deep in conversation about something.

An unwelcome bolt of jealousy stabs at my gut, and though I try to ignore it, I can still feel those nasty green claws in my gut an hour later when

Kerrie flops down next to me on the double chaise lounge. "I saw you with Leo," I say, the words coming of their own accord even though I know I'm indulging in word vomit. "You two looked cozy."

She smiles brightly. "He's a nice guy. I was thinking about what you said. That you thought we were dating." She lifts a shoulder, looking at me innocently. "I could see that."

My insides tighten up. "Not much sense starting something if you're leaving for California." I swallow. "Are you still planning on going?"

She tilts her head and crosses her arms as she looks down her nose at me. "Gee, Connor, I don't know. Should I stay here and date Leo? Or should I go take a fabulous job in LA with Delilah?"

"Kay..."

"Don't even," she says, lowering her voice so the others can't hear. "Do not play those games with me."

My shoulders sag. "I'm sorry. I really don't mean to."

Her mouth twists. "I believe you. I get it. And that's why I have to leave. Besides, there's no point staying. Leo's great, but he's not my guy."

"How do you know?"

She meets my eyes. "I know," she says aloud, but her tone says, "You're an idiot."

I stand up, suddenly feeling as if I've lost my grip on this conversation. "So when are you going to tell them?" I ask. "About LA, I mean."

She frowns, then sighs. "What the hell? I guess I should go ahead and tell them now."

―――――

Fifteen minutes later, I'm looking around the garden at a group of shocked faces, Pierce's most of all. "I'm going to miss you," he tells his little sister. "We've never lived that far apart."

"Um, Middle East?"

"That was a tour of duty," he tells her. "Not an address change."

"Maybe," she counters. "All I knew was that you were gone." At ten years younger than Pierce, I know she felt his absence deeply as a kid.

"We'll miss you," Jez puts in. "But if you're leaving us, I'm thrilled you'll be out there with Del. I miss her. More than that, I worry about her."

Kerrie waves a dismissive hand. "Worry no more. We'll have a blast. Girls gone wild in Hollywood."

Jez just stifles a laugh. It's Pierce who scowls and says, "How about we nix that idea?"

"Yeah," I say before I can stop myself. "Why don't we?"

Kerrie rolls her eyes. "Um, guys? It was a joke. That's not my thing. Or Del's."

"Kidding," I say, though of course I wasn't. Jealousy is an ugly mistress. And from the way Cayden is looking at me, I'm certain he knows that something's up.

"What?" I demand when we're standing together a few moments later.

For a moment, I think he's going to say something, but then Kerrie's phone rings.

She grabs it out of her back pocket, meets my eyes, and smiles.

For a minute or two, she just listens, her grin growing wider and wider. Then she ends the call and looks at all of us. "That was Noah," she says. "Not only does his gadget work like a charm, but he found the Carrington-Kohl information—and lots of other proprietor corporate files that he doubts were handed over voluntarily."

In other words, Michael Rollins is going down.

CHAPTER FOURTEEN

THE ROLLINS SITUATION is too big for
Blackwell-Lyon to handle, which is why the Justice
Department took over two weeks ago. Noah, Leo,
and I are consulting, but the Feds are on it, with
constant surveillance on Rollins as they build the
case, and an exit plan for Amy.

Moreover, the agents we're working with were
impressed enough with the job we did that I expect
we'll be getting some referrals for both on and
off-book jobs.

All of which is great.

And which begs the question of why I've been in
such a pissy mood for the last week. Except, of
course, I know why. It's because Kerrie flew to LA
eight days ago to find an apartment, and the cold

hard reality of her move is hitting me for the
first time.

I don't want her to go. But I can't ask her to stay.
Not unless I'm going to take our relationship further,
and I can't do that. Nothing has changed. I wanted
her before; I want her still. I was older than her
before; I'm older still.

I know the downside of that kind of age
difference, and not one goddamn thing has changed.
Nothing, that is, except this pit of loss and longing
that's growing in my gut. But that's selfish. And
where Kerrie is concerned I can't be selfish. I have to
think about what's best for her.

"You really think you're doing this for her?"
Cayden asks me when he finally calls me out on
being a moribund ass who's dragging down the mood
of everyone around me.

"I know I am. Do you think I'd let her out of my
sight if I wasn't positive?"

"Doing the right thing shouldn't make you so
miserable," he says. "Maybe you need to take another
look at the evidence. Maybe what you think is right is
all fucked up."

"It's not." I'm nothing if not firm in my resolve.

"You really think you're doing this for her?" he
asks again. This time, I don't bother answering.

He sighs. "So, what? That means there's someone else out there for you, too? Someone who fits you better than Kerrie? Because I've seen the two of you together, and you guys click."

We do. We really do.

"That's not the point," I tell him. "You know why we can't be together. I can't do that to her even if I love her. We're star-crossed."

"That is such bullshit." We're in my living room, and he's pacing in front of the window, a glorious panorama spread out behind him.

"How can you say that? You were there when Grandpa went downhill. You saw how much Gran gave up."

"*You* saw that," Cayden retorts. "You remembered how active Grandpa was and how much fun you two used to have throwing a ball around while I was off doing martial arts."

It's true. Cayden loved Grandpa, but I was the one who really spent time with him.

"You missed him and hated seeing him forced into bed after being so vibrant. And so you assumed that Gran was as laid flat by his decline as you were."

"Of course she was. The man had a heart attack. He was bedridden for years. How could you not see that?"

"I did," Cayden assures me. "I also saw a woman who loved her husband. Who read to him and laughed with him. Who watched movies and shared her life. I saw love, Connor. Do you think the fact that she couldn't hop on a plane and pop over to Rome changed that? For that matter, he never stopped her. She could have gone. She *chose* not to. She chose him. Because she loved him."

I say nothing.

He exhales, clearly frustrated. For a minute, I think he's done haranguing me. Then he narrows his eyes, studying me.

"What?"

"If I asked Kerrie if she thought there was someone out in the world better for you than her, what do you think she'd say?"

I scowl, but I also answer honestly. "She'd say no. But she's not thinking clearly."

"What gives you the right to decide for her?"

"Because I don't want her to be miserable."

He rubs his temples. "I love you, bro. But you know you're an idiot, right?"

"Dammit, Cay—"

"Should I sell my shares of Microsoft?" he blurts.

"What?" I'm completely baffled.

"How about Facebook? What should I buy this

year if I want to grow my savings by 150% in the next nine months?"

"Have you gone completely insane? What the hell are you talking about? How should I know what to do with your portfolio?"

"Oh, sorry." He flashes me a smug grin. "I thought you could see the future."

"It's not the same."

"Yeah," he says simply as he heads for my door. "It really is."

He leaves me alone, and though I know I should get up and do something—anything—all I can manage is to sit in my favorite chair and stare out at my view, watching as the sun sinks lower and lower in the sky.

A thousand thoughts race through my mind, but I can't wrap my head around any particular one. All I know is that I'm miserable. And that I love Kerrie. And that suddenly my phone is in my hand, and I'm dialing her number even though I have no idea what I'm going to say.

She answers on the first ring, her voice like a balm. "Hey, I was just thinking about you."

"I like the sound of that. Where are you?"

"I just got back in town."

"How was Los Angeles? Did you have fun?" I clutch my phone tighter. I really hope she hated it.

"I did. I think I'll like it out there. And Del and I have always gotten along fabulously, so work should be good."

I have to clear my throat before I can speak. "That's great," I finally manage to say, but my voice is flat. I can't conjure even an ounce of enthusiasm.

There's a pause. Then her voice comes across the line, soft and tentative. "Are you okay?"

"Sure. Just tired. The Feds. Work. Lots of stuff going on."

"Oh."

"You know what?" I blurt out before I even have time to think about my words. "Fuck that. I'm not tired and it's not work." The words flow like water, coming unbidden and unedited. But I don't want to stop them. They feel right. Like I've finally gotten out of my own way.

"Oh," she says again, but this time the word doesn't sound flat. It sounds hopeful.

"Don't go." I pour my heart and soul into those two words. "I know Del will be disappointed, and I know that LA might be fun, but we need you here. Who else is going to run the office? And keep us all in line?"

"Connor, please." Her voice is heavy. The sweet lilt fading.

I barrel on. "But that's only part of it. *I* need you. Hell, Kerrie, I love you."

Silence.

"Kerrie?"

"What are you saying?"

"I'm saying I've been an idiot. I'm saying I don't want to live without you." The words rush out of my heart and past my lips. "I'm saying that if you don't care about the years between us, then neither do I. What the hell is a number anyway? I was never good at math."

She laughs, the sound strangled, as if she's holding back tears.

"Kerrie? I know my timing sucks and Del will probably hate me. But please stay."

Again, there's silence. Except for a soft sound that might be crying.

"Kerrie? Baby, say something please."

"I love you, too," she whispers, her words melting my heart. "Now get your ass over here and kiss me."

CHAPTER FIFTEEN

I'M out the door in minutes, hauling ass toward her place. Now that I've made my decision—now that I've gotten my head out of my ass—I'm all in. Kerrie is mine, dammit, and we're moving forward together.

And as far as I'm concerned, together needs to start as soon as humanly possible.

It's not that far mileage-wise to her South Austin house from downtown, but traffic is a bitch in this town, and on top of that, I seem to hit every red light along the way.

I'm cursing Austin, city planners, and cars in general when my phone rings. I hit the button on my in-dash display to take it on speaker, assuming it's Kerrie.

It's not.

"Where are you?" Cayden asks, his voice tight.

"Heading to Kerrie's," I tell him. "I owe you a thanks. You were right. I've been an idiot. I'm—"

"Shut up and listen," he says. "I just sent you a text. Have you seen this?"

"I'm driving, remember?"

"It's important."

"Fuck." Since I'm at one of the damn red lights, I glance down at my phone, see that he's texted me an image, and push the button to transfer the picture to my console screen.

"Kerrie and Del," I say, glancing at the image of my girlfriend and her sister-in-law. "Not a bad picture." They're by the ocean, but traffic is moving again, so I take my eyes off the screen and continue down South First Street.

"Del sent it out over her Instagram feed," he says. "Some entertainment news agencies picked it up."

"This is all fascinating. Why do I care?"

"Because this is what she wrote." He starts to read. "So excited that my sister-in-law, Kerrie Blackwell, will be joining Team Delilah soon as my executive assistant, which pretty much means she'll be the boss of me. I'm so excited and can't wait for her to finish packing up her Austin house and move out here. And in case she looks familiar, Kerrie has been working for Blackwell-Lyon for years. That's the security company that helped me out a few years ago in Austin. So she's a tough cookie. Plus, her brother is the best. He'd have to be to be married to my sister. I'm so thrilled. Love you, K, and see you soon."

He stops reading and for a second there's silence. Honestly, I'm not sure what I'm supposed to say.

And then it hits me.

"The story was picked up?"

"Afraid so," my brother says.

"Where's Rollins?"

"The FBI went to pick him up, but he's bolted."

"Amy?"

"She's safe," Cayden says. "And when she poked around on his computer, she saw the picture. He's on his way to Austin. I'm certain of it."

"Fuck. Where are you? Where's Pierce? Leo?"

"Same as you. We're all heading to Kerrie's."

"You warned her?"

"Her phone's going straight to voicemail."

I bite back another curse. Hopefully she's just in the shower, and Rollins is still miles away. But I have a bad feeling.

"See you there."

I run the next three lights, pissing off the other drivers but not causing an accident, and when I screech to a halt in front of Kerrie's house, I'm relieved to see that there's no other car around. Pierce arrives only moments after me, looking as scared as I feel. I get it. She's my girlfriend, but she's his little sister. "She'll be fine," I say. Any other outcome is unacceptable.

"Any sign of Rollins?"

I shake my head. "I'm going in."

"I'm going around back," Pierce says. "Just in case."

I nod, then head to the front door. It's unlocked, which isn't a good sign, but when I step inside, my gun at the ready, Kerrie is alone.

"Thank God," I say, hurrying to her side as her eyes go wide. "Rollins—"

"—is very happy you're here." The voice is familiar, and I turn in time to see him emerge from the kitchen, his own weapon aimed at Kerrie. "You're just in time to watch her die."

I react without thinking, launching myself at her and knocking her to the ground just a split second before he fires. I hear the sharp report of the gun, then feel the burning impact in my leg. I smell gunpowder and blood, and I hear Kerrie's scream.

But I'm alive. For the moment. And so is Kerrie.

"Nobody screws me," Rollins growls, his voice seeming to come from underwater. I try to move, but it's not possible. But in my periphery, I can see him coming toward us, gun outstretched. I try to cover Kerrie, but I can't manage it. And then he raises his gun, and all I can think is that I can't let her die. But there's not a goddamn thing I can do except pray.

And then there's a loud *crack* and he flinches. Red blooms on his chest and he falls backward.

I hear Kerrie scream Pierce's name at the same time I see my friend burst in through the back door.

Everything blurs as a fresh wave of pain envelops me, but in the rising gray, I see Pierce take off his belt and tighten it around my leg. I hear the word *thigh*. I hear a siren.

Most of all, I hear Kerrie's voice telling me to stay with her.

"I love you," I whisper.

And as the world starts to turn gray, I see the fear on her face. I try to tell her it will be fine. No way am I leaving her now that we're together again. But somehow I can't make the words come.

That's okay, though. I know this isn't the end. On the contrary, it's just the beginning.

Because I'm not going anywhere. Not even if I

end up an old man with only one leg. No way am I pushing her away.

Not ever again.

EPILOGUE

Two months later

"HAPPY BIRTHDAY TO YOU! Happy birthday to you! Happy birthday, dear Kerrie ... Happy birthday to you!"

The horribly out of tune birthday serenade ends as I stand behind Kerrie, leaning on my cane as she makes a wish and blows out the candles. The cake is still in the nine-by-thirteen inch pan. A Betty Crocker yellow cake with Betty Crocker chocolate frosting. I made it myself, although according to Del I can't really say that I *made* it since it wasn't from scratch.

"You *combined* it," she'd insisted this morning when she stepped in as my much-needed kitchen

assistant. Only slightly younger than Kerrie, Delilah
has the bearing and sophistication of someone who's
grown up in the public eye. "And you baked it," she
added. "But you didn't make it."

She'd shrugged philosophically. "But you still get
credit for effort."

After the drama with Rollins—who died in the
hospital after falling into a coma—Kerrie had given
Del her regrets, electing to stay in Austin as our office
manager. And my girlfriend. As of today, we've been
living together for seven weeks and five days.

Today, I'm hoping to lock her in for a bit longer.
Like, say, a lifetime.

And I'm as nervous as a cat at a dog show.

As soon as the candles wink out, Kerrie beams
first at me, and then at the family and friends
gathered around us. Del, Cayden, Gracie, Jez, Pierce,
and Leo. Not to mention Amy, Noah Carter and his
wife Kiki, and at least a dozen more friends that
Pierce and I knew she'd want to celebrate this
day with.

At least, I hope that's the case.

"Can I cut the cake now?" She directs the
question at me, and I nod. Then immediately hold
up my hand and tell her to wait.

"Champagne," I say, then lean my cane against

the table as I limp toward the refrigerator. I should only need it for another month or two—the bullet did a number on my leg, but it's healing nicely—but in the meantime, Kerrie amuses herself by remarking what an old man I am every time I pass by.

I retaliate by threatening to withhold sex. At which point she has nothing but good things to say about my youth and prowess.

I return from the fridge with the champagne, which I open with a loud *pop*, followed by universal applause. Gracie passes around plastic flutes, and I pour for everyone.

"Fancy," Kerrie says with a grin. "Usually chocolate cake calls for cold milk."

"My girl deserves champagne," I say, moving beside her and kissing her head. I meet Del's eyes and find her grinning.

As for me, my stomach is in knots.

Kerrie seems entirely oblivious.

"Shall I just slice anywhere?" she asks. The cake is decorated with the words *Happy Birthday* over the number 26. Beneath the number is a little candy heart.

"That's your birthday girl slice," I say, pointing to the heart. "Cut a slice around that."

I hold my breath as she does, then slides it neatly out and puts it on her plate.

She starts to cut another slice, but I stop her. "Go ahead and see if you like it."

She frowns, looking around at the group. "I thought you were supposed to pass it around first."

I shake my head, looking at Del and Pierce for confirmation.

"He's right," Del says. "The birthday girl takes her wish-bite, then serves everyone else."

I watch as Kerrie looks at her brother, obviously confused. Pierce just shrugs. "I don't know the rules, and they sound pretty convinced."

"Family tradition," I say.

"Whatever." She takes her fork and starts to dig in, only to be stymied by something hard. "What the—"

I watch her face, seeing the exact moment when she realizes something is hidden in the cake. And then I see it go completely blank as she excavates the small metal box.

My stomach twists, suddenly fearful, because why isn't she smiling?

Then she opens the box, and I watch as joy floods her face, the emotion so palpable it makes me weak at the knees.

She looks at me, her lips moving, but she can't seem to form words.

I take the ring from her hand, then hold it out. A silent request for her ring finger.

When she extends her hand, I slip it on. The room is hushed, the silence rich with anticipation. "Yesterday we were fifteen years apart," I say. "But now it's only fourteen. So I had to pick today to ask you, Kerrie Blackwell, if you'll be my wife."

Tears trail down her cheeks as she nods. "Yes." Her voice is thick, and she tries again. "Oh, yes."

"I love you, Kay," I say as she launches herself into my arms.

"Love you, too, Old Man," she replies, then kisses me hard as our friends and family laugh and cheer, and I hold her tight, knowing that we're going to face our future together.

Meet Pierce in Lovely Little Liar

She's not the woman I thought … but dammit, she's the woman I want.

I never thought of myself as cynical, but getting dumped at the altar changes a man.

Now, I'm all about my job. About building my business and getting on with my life. Don't get me wrong; I still love women. I love the way they look. The way they smell. The way they feel. Especially the way they feel. And I've pretty much made it my mission to give each and every woman who shares my bed the ride of her life.

But getting close? Getting serious? Giving a woman my trust again? Yeah, that's not going to happen.

Or so I thought.

Then I met her. It's funny how things can change in a heartbeat. How one case of mistaken identity can change everything. But there she was, all business and completely uninterested in me. And damned if I didn't want her. Crave her.

Most of all, I wanted to help her. To keep her and her sister safe. But the more I get to know her, the more I want her. The whole package. The complete woman.

And the miracle is that she wants me, too.

Trouble is, we've both been burned before. Now, I know one thing for certain—the only way that we'll survive the heat that crackles between us is if we both find the courage to leap into the fire together.

Lovely Little Liar is a novella originally published as Bitch Slap. Minor edits, such as expanded scenes, have been made to this book.

Meet Cayden in Pretty Little Player

Bedroom games are fine ... but I need a woman who won't play with my heart.

After years in the military, I've faced down a lot of things, and there's not much I shy away from. Except relationships. Because when you catch your wife in bed with another man, that tends to sour even the most hardened man against women.

When I was hired to keep surveillance on a woman with a checkered past, I went into the job anticipating the worst. But what I found was a woman who turned my head. Who made my blood heat and my body burn. A woman who made me feel alive again.

A woman who was nothing like what I expected, but everything I wanted. A woman who, it turned out, needed my protection. And wanted my touch.

And as the world fell out from under us, and everything I thought I knew shifted, there was only one reality I could hold onto—that the more I got to know her, the more I wanted her.

But if I'm going to make her mine, I'll have to not only keep her safe, I'll have to prove to her that I've conquered my own fears and doubts. That I'm done looking into the past, and that all I want is a future —with her.

WHO'S YOUR MAN OF THE MONTH?

When a group of fiercely determined friends realize their beloved hang-out is in danger of closing, they take matters into their own hands to bring back customers lost to a competing bar. Fighting fire with a heat of their own, they double down with the broad shoulders, six-pack abs, and bare chests of dozens of hot, local guys who they cajole, prod, and coerce into auditioning for a Man of the Month calendar.

But it's not just the fate of the bar that's at stake. Because as things heat up, each of the men meets his match in this sexy, flirty, and compelling binge-read romance series of twelve novels releasing every other week from *New York Times* bestselling author J. Kenner.

"With each novel featuring a favorite romance trope —beauty and the beast, billionaire bad boys, friends to lovers, second chance romance, secret baby, and more—[the Man of the Month] series hits the heart and soul of romance." *New York Times* bestselling author Carly Phillips

**Down On Me - Hold On Tight - Need
You Now
Start Me Up - Get It On - In Your Eyes
Turn Me On - Shake It Up - All Night Long
In Too Deep - Light My Fire - Walk
The Line**

Bar Bites: A Man of the Month Cookbook

CHARISMATIC. DANGEROUS. SEXY AS HELL.
MEET THE MEN OF STARK SECURITY.
COMING IN 2019

Stark Security, a high-end, high-tech, no-holds barred security firm founded by billionaire Damien Stark and security specialist Ryan Hunter has one mission: Do whatever it takes to protect the innocent. Only the best in the business are good enough for Stark Security.

Men with dangerous skills.

Men with something to prove.

Brilliant, charismatic, sexy as hell, they have no time for softness—they work hard and they play harder. They'll take any risk to get the job done.

But what they won't do is lose their hearts.

Shattered With You
Broken With You
Ruined With You

Meet Damien Stark

Only his passion could set her free...

The Original Trilogy
Release Me
Claim Me
Complete Me
And Beyond...
Anchor Me
Lost With Me
DAMIEN

Meet Damien Stark in the award-winning &
international bestselling series that started it all.

The Stark Saga by J. Kenner

ABOUT THE AUTHOR

J. Kenner (aka Julie Kenner) is the *New York Times,
USA Today, Publishers Weekly, Wall Street Journal*
and #1 International bestselling author of over one
hundred novels, novellas and short stories in a
variety of genres.

JK has been praised by
Publishers Weekly as an author
with a "flair for dialogue and
eccentric characterizations" and
by *RT Bookclub* for having
"cornered the market on sinfully
attractive, dominant antiheroes
and the women who swoon for them." A six-time
finalist for Romance Writers of America's prestigious
RITA award, JK took home the first RITA trophy
awarded in the category of erotic romance in 2014
for her novel, *Claim Me* (book 2 of her Stark Saga)
and the RITA trophy for *Wicked Dirty* in the same
category in 2017.

In her previous career as an attorney, JK worked

as a lawyer in Southern California and Texas. She currently lives in Central Texas, with her husband, two daughters, and two rather spastic cats.

Visit her website at www.juliekenner.com to learn more and to connect with JK through social media!

CPSIA information can be obtained
at www.ICGtesting.com
Printed in the USA
LVHW041510111019
633943LV00011B/430/P